W9-CSX-166

shadowed summer

shadowed summer

– By –

SAUNDRA MITCHELL

&

DELACORTE PRESS

Published by Delacorte Press
an imprint of Random House Children's Books
a division of Random House, Inc.
New York

This is a work of fiction. Names, characters, places, and incidents either are the
product of the author's imagination or are used fictitiously. Any resemblance to
actual persons, living or dead, events, or locales is entirely coincidental.

Copyright © 2009 by Saundra Walters

All rights reserved.
Delacorte Press and colophon are registered trademarks of Random House, Inc.

Visit us on the Web! www.randomhouse.com/teens

Educators and librarians, for a variety of teaching tools,
visit us at www.randomhouse.com/teachers

Library of Congress Cataloging-in-Publication Data
Mitchell, Saundra.
Shadowed Summer / Saundra Mitchell. — 1st ed.
p.   cm.
Summary: In the small town of Ondine, Louisiana, fourteen-year-old Iris uncovers
family secrets when she conjures up the ghost of a boy missing for decades and
decides to solve the mystery of his disappearance.
ISBN: 978-0-385-73571-1 (hardcover)
ISBN: 978-0-385-90560-2 (glb edition)
[1. Ghosts—Fiction. 2. Secrets—Fiction. 3. Louisiana—Fiction.]
I. Title II. Title: Shadowed Summer
PZ7.M6953 Sh 2009
[Fic]—dc22
2008010021

The text of this book is set in 11-point Sabon.

Book design by Trish P. Watts

Printed in the United States of America

10 9 8 7 6 5 4 3 2 1

First Edition

Random House Children's Books supports the First Amendment
and celebrates the right to read.

For Jason and Wendi—
You make all things possible.

&

In memory of Matt and Braden—
Nothing gold can stay.

chapter one

&

Nothing ever happened in Ondine, Louisiana, not even the summer Elijah Landry disappeared. That was an incident; and being specific, it was "The Incident with the Landry Boy."

Since he never was found, it gave me and my best friend, Collette, something to wonder about, and in Ondine, wondering was about all we had to do.

According to the sign out by the highway, Ondine was home to 346 GOOD PEOPLE AND 3 CRANKY OLD COOTS and was a good place to live, but that was a lie.

Ben Duvall's daddy hung the sign out during the evacuation. Ondine was on the way to Baton Rouge, and people seemed to think if we touched up our paint, some of New Orleans's storm refugees would stay and make this home.

Nobody stayed longer than it took to get supper, and why would they?

1

We had a gas station and a Red Stripe grocery store that rented DVDs for three dollars a night—they didn't have anything good.

Collette's mama regularly lost her temper over the broken grill at the diner. And Father Rey was brimstone enough that even our Baptists would sit in his pews instead of driving a town over to worship, especially if he trotted out the sermons about loving the sinner and hating the sin.

That was entertainment, and that was all we had.

When school was in, there was maybe ten of us, and we rode a bus forty minutes to St. Amant. That was different, at least, but come summer, all we had was stale movies from the Red Stripe, extra Masses, and making stuff up.

Since we couldn't drive yet, me and Collette did a whole lot of making stuff up.

Well, we used to, anyway.

Sometimes we'd be knights. It didn't matter that knights were supposed to be boys; we could ride horses and swing swords if we wanted to. Sometimes we'd be witches, or elementals, or whatever good thing we thought up or got from our library books.

We found magic everywhere, in the trees and the wind, in teacups and rainstorms. We were bigger than Ondine, better than the ordinary people who came and went and never stopped to wonder what lay underneath the church's tiger lilies to give them such bloodred hearts.

Nobody but us seemed to wonder or bother or ask about anything, and we felt strangled being the only ones. When we were twelve, Collette pricked her finger to make a vow that she'd get us out of Ondine as soon as she got her license. It made me a little dizzy to see the red beading up

2

on her skin, but I let her poke me, too. Anybody could make a promise; we had to bind ours with a spell.

But that was used-to-be, back when we had a New Orleans to run away to, before the storm, before we turned fourteen. Fourteen changed everything.

Collette was first; she was born in February. She developed first, too. She wanted everybody to think she was embarrassed when her bra strap kept slipping down her arm, but I knew her better than that. Every time, her dark eyes darted, looking to see who'd noticed.

I turned fourteen in May, and I was just fine with the way things were. I didn't need a bra, or want one, either. Ondine wasn't any bigger, we still couldn't go anywhere, and driving was two years out yet. Our games suited me fine.

Collette, though, rewrote them some. We never played *only* witches anymore; somebody had to have a sweetheart. Or we had to taint apples with twisted love spells. Most important, though, we couldn't play out where the boys could see us and throw rocks.

We *used* to throw rocks back. But making up imaginary worlds was more important to me than arguing with Collette about her being boy-crazy, so I just went along.

After Mass, we invaded the cemetery row by row, back to the old side of the yard.

"Where y'at?" Collette asked, and helped me onto Jules Claiborne's crypt.

It was just a grayish slab box, maybe six feet long. Its top was pocked from rain, rough and nubbly, and it made our jeans catch on the surface.

Folding my legs up, I settled on the stone. "I'm fine. How are you?"

3

Collette looked down to make her dark curls fall in her eyes. She had good hair. There was a springy kind of coil to it that made me want to reach out and tug it, just to watch it bounce back. I always wanted hair like that, even though she said I didn't—too much trouble. I'd argue about it, though. She'd never had to suffer straight and stringy dish-water blond.

"I'm all right. But listen."

Collette had a new spell to cast; she glared and threw her hands out to catch lightning, her hair rising like a midnight halo around her head as she tried to call the spirits of the dead.

I cupped my hands behind my ears and closed my eyes. At first, I smelled more than I heard. Water and stone, over-perfumed magnolias ripening with the heat. A bite of bitter cypress swirled around under that, and my stomach turned before I managed to pay attention with my ears.

To be honest, I didn't hear anything unusual: a little bit of wind, some birds, a couple of spring peepers confused about the time of day, and cicadas. Those rattled and hummed, ticking like a windup clock, then exploding with a maraca burst before starting over again.

But Collette wouldn't make a point of listening to them. Since I didn't hear anything new, I faked it. Trying to sound spooky, I barely whispered, "What is that?"

"They're trying to talk to us," Collette said, stroking the crypt top with both hands. "We're the only ones who can hear them, Iris."

I nodded, getting into the feel of something mystical, even if I didn't know what it was. Possibility prickled at the back of my neck; it made my heart beat fast in anticipation.

A copper tang spread on my tongue, a taste that made me go all tight inside, waiting for something to happen.

Still low, I just breathed out, "Ohhh . . ."

"Can you hear them?" She always insisted that winds shifted for *us*, winds the rest of Ondine never felt at all.

"Uh-huh," I lied.

Collette pushed up suddenly. Turning like a weather vane, she pointed at the next crypt over and fell into her best spell-casting voice. "We have to cover their bones. You go lay over there."

In a second, I'd hopped down from Jules Claiborne's granite death-bed, and grunted my way onto his wife Cecily's. My pants caught on the frills edging her slab, but I didn't even wince when I felt the denim tear. My jeans were already short by a half an inch; a hole in the knee wouldn't matter much. Besides, the dead were talking; I wanted to listen.

Spreading myself out, I closed my eyes. "What now?"

Collette hummed, low and mysterious. "Breathe real slow, only as much as you have to, and wait. You have to feel kind of dead, so they aren't too scared to come close."

My heartbeat rattled in time with the cicada calls, and I could hardly hold still. Those old souls, out of their skins and not quite to heaven, seemed to swarm around us. I didn't have to work hard to control my breath; fear and excitement did that for me.

Cecily was coming into my body. She'd use my legs to stand on, run my hands through my hair, and walk off— probably into the bayou. I'd turn up missing, not even a drop of me left on my pillow. It'd be "The Incident with the Rhame Girl." I'd be trapped forever, screaming where nobody could hear me, right inside my own self.

The air felt hot and wet but far away, like the warmth thrown off a campfire. Laid out on Cecily's slab, I should have been sweating and ready for some lemonade, but all I had in me was cold.

Voices scratched and rattled in my ears; it wasn't a pretty magic running through my veins just then. It tasted storm-dark. Rain tears wet my skin.

I managed to turn my head, but Collette didn't see me. She looked peaceful, floating on a stone that was as still as her body. For a moment, I was sure she was dead. My chest ached, bound with a scream I couldn't get out, and that was when someone touched my hair.

A creamy flash passed in front of me, leaving the shadow of a face made up mostly of dark eyes. Wind kissed my ear, cool and soft, and I heard a voice. It sounded like clover tastes, green and new and sweet.

"Where y'at, Iris?"

chapter two

&

Quick as that, I wasn't afraid of Cecily Claiborne any-more; she was just a fairy scare, one I conjured up all by myself, but that boy's voice whispering in my ear—that was *real*.

My feet sank into the soft ground before I realized I'd moved, and I scrambled toward Collette. "Did you hear that?"

Sitting up, Collette made a face at me. "You're supposed to—"

"I'm serious!" Grabbing her arm, I yanked her up farther as I craned around, looking for the boy. I didn't see more than a spot of pale, but it seemed like he should be long and tall, slipping fast through the stones and into the woods.

"What's wrong with you?" Collette huffed.

The sky started to groan, promising rain anytime, but it was still light enough that Collette should have seen him or heard him, and I got a fresh chill when it was plain she didn't.

Swallowing hard, I let go of her arm and turned around and around, searching for proof I didn't have. We'd done so much pretending that I didn't know how to convince her that this time, something *had* happened. My daddy would have said that was the curse of a liar.

Giving up, I said, "It's fixing to rain; we better go."

Collette could fill up a sigh with more disgust than anybody I knew, but she slid from Jules's slab even as she rolled her eyes. With a flourish, she started for the gate without looking back, as if I wouldn't have known how put-upon she was without the big exit.

Anyway, I didn't care, because my ear still tingled from that secret whisper, and I wanted to go home.

ℰ

After we abandoned the cemetery, Collette and I tried to figure out what to do next. For a while, we stood on my back porch and watched the Delancie brothers blow up the creek again.

Through the trees and scrub, we saw two auburn heads bobbing. They'd stay put for a second, then run off before a wake of white water exploded toward the sky.

I scratched my cheek and made a guess. "Sounds like cherry bombs."

"You think?"

"Yeah, they ain't as loud as them M-80s they got last summer."

The thick air rippled with another explosion. I felt the

snap in my ears and on my skin and followed the sound as it rolled away in the rain.

Way off, a siren started, and the Delancies bolted for their house, cussing. I'd learned some of my best words from them.

With the show over, Collette raised her umbrella and hopped a step. "Let's go to the Red Stripe and get some RCs."

My stomach sank. "I don't have any money."

Collette shrugged. "I do. I'll lend you."

"Well, I do have some! But your mama gives 'em to us free!" Right out of the fountain at the diner, as much as we could drink.

"And then we have to bus tables," she reminded me. "And put up with Rooster and Mama digging into our conversations whenever she wants and taking out the trash and whatever else. I don't think so."

I frowned. "But they're free."

"Uh-uh, they just don't cost *money.*"

Since she'd made up her mind, she started walking. I scrambled after her, circling and dogging her steps. Slow with the weight of dread, I yanked her attention back to the cemetery.

"I really did hear something," I said. Sweetening the pot, I added, "I saw something, too."

Collette's brows disappeared under a fringe of frizz. "You did not!" But the rain had washed the snit off of her. I crossed my chest with my fingers three times: one for God, one for Jesus, and one for the Holy Ghost. "Swear I did."

"Well?"

"I saw a boy, and he asked me how I was." I shrugged, ducking when she whipped around to walk in front of me.

"Which wouldn't be anything, I guess, except then he wasn't there."

"What'd he look like?" Collette sounded exactly like I did when I was just going along, only in my opinion she wasn't as good at it.

I brushed past her. "Brown hair, brown eyes. I only saw him for a second, but he was there, Collette. He leaned right in and said"—for demonstration, I leaned, too, trying to imitate the voice still ringing in my head—" 'Where y'at, Iris?' "

Shaking the umbrella, Collette stopped in front of the Red Stripe. "That's a dumb thing for a ghost to say."

She knew I could make up better stories than that, and I waited about forever for her to admit it. When she finally did, she didn't bother saying sorry or anything, she just shrugged and leaned back against the door to open it. "He didn't tell you his name?"

I shook my head.

"He was probably scared," Collette said, then walked inside.

The Red Stripe didn't have any air-conditioning, just an old black fan on the front counter and the back door open all the way. Going in there felt like putting on a cloak of steam and dust.

I headed down the narrow aisle toward the soda coolers. "Didn't seem like it to me. He sounded like anybody. I bet he woulda talked more if I hadn't spooked."

With a suffering sigh, Collette followed. Every other step, she raised up on her toes, peering over the tops of tin cans arranged by color.

The owner, Mr. Ourso, had a lot of time on his hands, so

sometimes he'd stack the groceries alphabetical. Sometimes he did them by size—you never knew until you got there.

"What were you scared of, anyway? It's not like we ain't been looking for haunts since we . . ." She stepped up, peeked, then finished her sentence with, "Shhh!"

"I'd like to see you—"

"Shh!" Collette plastered her hand on my head to keep me out of sight as she turned the corner. "Hi, Ben."

I crabbed away, making faces at a bag of butter-flavored pretzels. Just to be annoying, I called out, "Hey, Ben!"

She was making goo-goo eyes at Ben Duvall, the whole blond reason we had to come to the Red Stripe. Until he started working there two days a week, the fountain at the diner had been good enough.

"Hey, Iris," he said. Then he started telling Collette about his new model.

I crept to the freezers in back to make sure I didn't accidentally pinch Collette for being stupid over him. The way she nodded when he talked about his model of the Eiffel Tower, you would have thought he was building a life-sized one in his backyard.

We'd known Ben all our lives, and he wasn't that interesting. He liked building models and reading comic books, and he used to pull our hair in church. The only thing worth knowing about him was that his mama named him after a Shakespeare character—Benvolio—and he took the job unpacking for Mr. Ourso when she came down with breast cancer.

Snatching a couple of Neapolitan ice cream sandwiches, I walked as loud as I could right past them. "Anyway, so I guess we can call up the dead tomorrow or something."

A just-smacked blush darkened Collette's cheeks. "Whatever, Iris."

"Calling up the dead?" Ben stuffed a box knife into his red work apron and looked back and forth between us. He whispered, just loud enough for us to hear, "Y'all been witching?"

Collette opened her mouth, but I talked first, and louder. "Nope. We're psychic. Lost souls talk the loudest in the graveyard."

"Really?"

"It's just a game we play," Collette said. She squeezed a can of mandarin oranges so hard her knuckles went pale.

I waved my ice cream at them as I backed toward the register. "No, it's for real. She just doesn't want to brag, is all."

Ben wavered; he had sense enough to realize Collette didn't want to talk about it, but I guess curiosity won. He cut me a glance. "How about you show me sometime?"

At that, Collette's blush faded and she nodded. Her voice went soft, and she took a deep breath, the kind that let her bra strap peek from under her shirt when she exhaled. "I will, if you want."

"Okay, then," Ben said, his face lighting with a sudden smile.

Rolling the mandarin orange can between her palms, Collette drifted toward me, smiling like a debutante. "You should come over to my house so I can teach you the right way to listen."

I paid for my ice cream in change and left before she promised to teach him all our secret spells, too.

꒰

A wave of fried green pepper and onion perfume hit my nose as I came in the door.

Standing over the stove, Daddy held a pan out to keep it from spattering on his crisp blue work shirt. The back read JESSEE'S TOOL AND DIE, and the patch over his pocket said JACK.

When he made dinner, it was musical. Pots clanged, oil sizzled, and sausages whistled just a little when he popped them with the tip of a knife. Under it all, I could hear him humming.

Gathering forks and spoons for just two places, I swayed in time to his music. It was just me and him—Mama died in a car accident when I was three. And since he worked graveyard at the machine shop, he was a familiar stranger.

I stole looks at him while I set the table. He kept his hair slicked back, not so wet that light would shine on it, just enough to keep it neat. His hazel eyes sparkled, and when he stood up straight, I could tip my head back and see nothing but the silver scar on the underside of his chin. It wasn't like I could forget what he looked like, but it never hurt to make sure. All my mama was to me was a memory of long brown hair and a red sundress.

When I finished setting the table, I sat down and worked on folding our paper-towel napkins into perfect triangles. He shifted pans back and forth; I kept my eyes down. I wanted to ask him about things belonging to the next world, but I needed to start with something solid.

"Collette's sweet on Ben Duvall," I said, carefully placing my spoon and knife on top of the napkin. "She says he's pretty."

"I reckon if I was Ben Duvall, I'd be insulted." Daddy

rumbled with a laugh, turning to put a big black skillet on the table.

Together we bowed our heads, and Daddy said a short prayer, picking up his napkin after the amen. "I hope you're not of the same mind."

I stuck out my tongue. "Nasty, Daddy."

"That's my girl." He scooped a heap of fried potatoes onto my plate, then chased a sausage around the inside of the skillet to catch it for me. "Luke's going to have his hands full if he ends up with a daughter-in-law like Collette."

Making another, more horrified, face, I smeared some ketchup onto the edge of my plate. "She doesn't want to marry him, she just likes looking at him."

Daddy laughed and changed the subject. "Did you catch yourself any pixies today?"

I stopped, my fork halfway to my mouth, and shook my head. "No, but we weren't trying."

"Mind your elbows. It's probably for the best," Daddy said. "I've got enough cut out feeding the two of us."

Most days, it made me glad that Daddy went along. I knew he didn't like the magic games. He believed in God, and the church, and the devil, too, but he didn't nag about it, not like Collette's mama did. Course, he didn't know we'd moved to the cemetery, either.

I finished my bite, then took a drink of lemonade to wash it down. "Do you believe in ghosts?"

Daddy waved his fork. "Everything I've ever seen had an explanation, but it's a big world, and I haven't seen everything yet."

That didn't help. I tried again. "So there *could* be ghosts. You just haven't seen any."

Daddy squinted at me. "What have you been up to?"

"Nothing," I mumbled, and stuffed my mouth with sausage, taking advantage of manners to stay silent for a minute. "I just thought I saw something in the graveyard."

"I don't want y'all messing around up in there."

Frustrated, I put my spoon down heavy. "We weren't messing; we were just looking at the names."

"Try the phone book," he said, slicing into his potatoes. "It's about the same."

"Daddy!"

Satisfied he'd made his point, he turned his plate and finally asked, "What kind of something?"

"I don't know, just something. It was there, and then it wasn't."

"Was it a grave lantern?" Daddy asked. "They get restless when a storm's coming."

Everybody else called it fox fire, or swamp lights, or *les feux follets* if they felt fancy. It was all the same—a phantom glow that wandered off the bayou on humid, heat-lightning nights. Daddy, though, called it grave lanterns. Just the sound of it made my skin crawl—grave lanterns, like the cold light of an ember carried up from hell.

I shook my head. "No, not that."

Ticking his fork against his plate, Daddy etched out an uncomfortable sound, his way of thinking out loud. "Maybe a rabbit or a bird, then."

"It was a *person*," I blurted out. I dropped my hands on the table so hard that our dishes chattered. "It was a boy, and he said my name, and then he was gone."

Daddy quirked a brow. "I hope *he* wasn't pretty."

"It's not funny."

15

"Iris," he said, standing to clear his plate. "It seems to me that if there were ghosts, the last place you'd find them is a cemetery."

Blankly, I stared at him. "But why?"

"That's a place for the living to go to remember. By the time we put somebody in the ground, their soul is long gone."

"Oh."

He made sense. If I'd passed on but wanted to stay, it sure wouldn't be at my crypt. I'd want to be right there in my own kitchen, listening to Daddy sing whenever I wanted.

"I gotta get going, baby girl," he said, dumping his dishes in the sink. "Make sure you clean up, all right?"

I stared down at my dinner; the shimmer of grease turned my stomach all of a sudden. "When are we gonna get a new dishwasher?"

"Just as soon as they grow on trees."

&

Half pink, half blue, my bedroom was caught somewhere between being little and being grown. Ballerinas danced in watercolor on one wall; magazine posters of pop stars gazed down from the other. Because of them, I had to get dressed in the bathroom.

Tugging my robe closed, I wedged myself behind the white painted desk that had been mine since kindergarten. My knees brushed the underside of it as I searched the mess on top. Hiding with a stack of paperbacks, I found what I was looking for: my spellbook.

Collette had one just like it, spiral-bound with a heavy

black cover. We figured nobody'd care about a school note-book enough to look in it. Just in case somebody did, though, we wrote a curse on the first page: *Abandon this book now, or get a bleeding wart on your eyeball for every spell you read.*

Part of me hoped the next time I saw Ben Duvall, he'd be wearing bandages and sunglasses.

Uncapping a pen with my teeth, I flipped past the were-wolf potion and the potion for everlasting life to find a blank page. I'd planned to write out *How to Talk to the Dead,* but after that talk at dinner, I didn't want to any-more. Still, I had to mark down something.

Daddy liked to say it was all right to talk to God, but you were a little touched if God talked back. Remembering that made it easy to mark down our latest discovery. I finished it as quick as I could, then shoved the book into the drawer, pen and all.

Unlike the other spells we had, I didn't reckon we'd be using *How to Make Yourself Go Crazy* very often.

chapter three

&

The sun hadn't risen high enough to blaze through my window, but it was already strangling hot in my room. My nightgown stuck to me, peeling from my skin with a tickle. I scraped my feet as I walked, trying not to move overmuch.

Sleep held on, calling me back to bed—maybe back to something different and good, like the dream where I could hold out my hands and just fly. As fine as sleeping sounded on a hot day, you could lose a whole summer like that if you weren't careful.

The frigid prickle of a cold shower felt good for the first couple of minutes. After that, it was just cold. I slipped into my room to grab some clothes, my chilly skin already warming back up to Louisiana humid. New sweat started on my upper lip, and I frowned at my dresser. If it was decent, I would have gone naked. Since it wasn't, I picked out shorts and an old T-shirt.

18

As I skulked into the hallway, something nagged at me, like I'd left something behind. Fingering through my clothes, I found everything I needed, but I looked back anyway.

There on my desk, on top of everything, was my spell-book.

In Collette's house, that would have been a sign to start beating her baby brother—the one we called Rooster, since he up and decided to have red hair when the rest of the family was brunet. I was an only child, though, and Daddy was sound asleep, so something I put in my drawer should have stayed there.

I stood in the doorway, staring. It was long enough that I wanted to dig a sweater from the back of my closet to chase off new goose bumps.

It took me a couple tries to touch the cover, which meant I felt pretty dumb when it felt like a spiral-bound notebook. It could have given me a static shock, at least. Bracing the edge with my thumb, I flipped from the front to the back, making sure it was my book. Everything looked the same.

Wound up tight and afraid of my own room, I told myself out loud, "I'm closing my book in this drawer, and I'm not imagining that." I took a deep breath and shoved it back in the desk.

Then I ran.

&

Daddy was going to be awful surprised when he woke up. I'd folded every towel in the house, swept the kitchen, and even mopped a little bit before switching to the push vacuum in the living room.

Whipping myself to a sweat in spite of the air conditioner, I felt my room above me, like it could sink through the ceiling and sit on my shoulders. I didn't like thinking that someone—some *thing*—had been messing around in there while I was asleep.

I could avoid going up there during the day, but I'd have to sleep in my own bed sooner or later. I had to figure out how to cure a book-moving ghost.

Giving the rug one more sweep, I dragged the vacuum back to its closet and started for the staircase. All of a sudden, it was hard to breathe, and my fingers didn't even feel like they belonged to my hands when I grabbed the rail. I'd only made it up three steps when the phone rang and nearly made me lose my balance. For a crazy second, I wondered if it would be the boy from the cemetery on the line, asking me how I was, but it was only Collette.

"Meet me at our place in fifteen minutes," she said, talking fast, like somebody might be listening. "Just bring you."

I wrinkled my nose and leaned against the wall. "What else would I bring?"

Collette sounded exasperated. "I don't know. Anything. Whatever!"

"You're talking crazy, Collette. I hope you know that."

"Just bring you and get on over there, all right?" A rattly static sound filled my ear. I could hear her talking to somebody but she sounded far away. It got quiet again right after that; then her voice cleared. "It's *important*, Iris."

&

20

A half hour later, I wandered around Jules Claiborne's crypt alone, searching for a little bit of shade. I felt like I could have peeled the skin off my shoulders in crispy strips. The puddle of sweat at the small of my back made me shudder.

Collette hadn't shown up.

Just a touch bitter, I kicked at the edge of the crypt. I should have stayed home in the first place. Haunt in my desk drawer or not, at least the living room was air-conditioned, and Daddy had a case of root beer in the fridge. My mouth went wet just thinking about it.

I'd decided to leave and was at the gate when I saw Collette finally coming down the road. I went to yell something mean at her when I spotted Ben. He straggled along, carrying a box and looking at his sneakers.

Rankled down to my bones, I gritted my teeth and held the gate closed. Fine if she wanted to be late on me, but I wasn't about to let her bring somebody else to *our* place. "Since when was there thirty minutes in fifteen?" I asked.

"Sorry," Collette said, slowing to fall in step with Ben. "We had to stop and get something."

"Hey," Ben mumbled, hoisting a long white box to prove their errand.

I glared at Collette, leaning into the gate until the notched iron nipped at my thigh. She didn't even realize I was mad; I itched to slap her. "You coulda said that on the phone."

"It was a surprise!"

Ben tucked his box under his arm and trailed away from the gate. "Uh . . . I think I hear my mama calling. I'm gonna go see what she wants."

21

He didn't hear her, unless she'd followed him four blocks with a bullhorn, but it was a good excuse. The Duvalls had their faults—they all had a touch of stuck-up, because they had money left over from the Gold Coast days in Ascension Parish—but nobody could call them stupid.

Disappointment ran across Collette's face, breaking her mouth and eyes to downward curves. A split second later, she wheeled around, growling under her breath, "You tell him to come back!"

"No, ma'am." To make my point, I rattled the gate between us. She could pick making kissy face with Ben or reaching out for the otherworld with me; it was that simple.

Balling her fists like she had to keep them from strangling me on their own accord, Collette leaned closer. "Dummy, he's got a witchboard! Tell him to come back!"

My resolve unstuck itself right then and there.

Collette's mama and my daddy didn't put their feet down much, but they both did when we wanted a Ouija board. Playing with one was too much like Satanism.

Peeling my fingers off the gate, I gave Collette one last, hard look, then stepped aside. "I don't think that was your mama, Ben. Come on back."

⅋

"You're not supposed to do it by yourself," Ben said, unfolding the board between us. "You need at least two, to keep from being possessed."

Nodding at this wisdom, we watched as Ben shook the pointer out of its red velvet bag. His witchboard was even better than we hoped.

Instead of cardboard and plastic, like the kind that came from the store, Ben's was made of wood—mahogany, with light pine letters set right into the top. When I touched the pointer, it was warm and buttery. And heavy, too—alive and full of witch fire.

Secretly, I admired Ben a little more for owning something so fine and rare, but only a little.

"Where'd you get this?" I whispered.

"It was my nonna's," he said, rubbing the board with a fluffy cloth square. "And it was her nonna's; she brought it over when she came from Italy."

Generations of Ben's family had passed the board on? Most people had only bothered to bring a family Bible over from Europe. That they brought this made me twice as impressed.

"All right, everybody has to promise not to push," Collette said. She put the pointer in the middle of the board, then tapped the edge with her finger to test it. It took barely anything to slide to the spot on the bottom that said ADDIO. Since I recognized sì and NO on the top, I guessed *addio* meant "goodbye."

"I'm not going to push," I promised quietly as I put my fingers down.

"What should we ask first?" Collette whispered.

Rolling his head back to stare at the sky, as if the answer would be written in the clouds, Ben thought about it for a minute. "Is anybody listening?"

The pointer didn't move.

Every second lasted a whole afternoon, and I felt old and wound up when I finally said, "Maybe we should try something else."

Nudging me, Collette lifted her fingers and rubbed the sweat from them. "You should ask if he's here."

"Who?" Ben smiled, his eyes flicking at me, then back at her.

My face went hot. I guess I deserved it, for going out of my way to embarrass Collette at the Red Stripe the day before, but still. If I'd wanted to mention being a little crazy, I would have brought it up myself. "Nobody."

"She saw a ghost, right here." Collette nodded toward Claire's crypt. "Well, over there, really. He came right up close and said her name."

Ben's mouth dropped open. "Really?"

Shrugging, I gritted my teeth. I hadn't had a chance to tell her I must have made it all up, but, selfishly, I didn't want to give Ben a reason to take his beautiful witchboard home. "Yeah."

"Then we should try him," Ben said. His eyes were cornflower blue; I'd never noticed that before.

The pointer slipped around under my fingers, and I watched the tendons flickering in my wrist. Out of curiosity, I pushed real light. Even though the pointer moved, my muscles hardly told on me; Collette and Ben didn't seem to notice. "I guess we could try."

Settling in, I took a deep breath. My family had all kinds of haunts. My great-aunt Corinne saw her dead mama in a turned-off television, and Daddy's cousin Paul always dreamed a white dove right before somebody died.

I knew from a real haunt and what Daddy had said about ghosts and graveyards rolled around in my head, so I didn't feel bad making one up. We were the living remembering the dead, after all.

Closing my eyes, I whispered in my best magic voice, "You out there? It's me, Iris."

Sweat trickled down my back. I waited for a minute before pushing. Peeking through my lashes, I tried to look blind as I slowly guided the arrow to sì.

Collette murmured in amazement, and Ben whispered, "It's working."

I slipped into a medium's skin, rolling my head around to loosen my neck before picking another question that sounded séance-proper. "You're here with us now?" I tugged on the pointer, then slid it right back to sì.

"We should ask something we already know, as a test." The sweltering heat carried Collette and Ben's electricity, a little storm of excitement brewing on top of Jules's crypt.

Collette smacked her lips. She always did when she was thinking. She said, "Are you a boy or a girl?"

Since it was my show and all, I decided my ghost didn't want to answer Collette. The pointer sat still on the sì, unmoving until Ben suggested I try asking.

"Maybe they only like you?"

Trying not to smile, I nodded and repeated the question. It was harder to spell out words with my eyes mostly closed, so my ghost said he was a boz instead of a boy, but that was close enough.

Another electric wave flickered through Ben and Collette, and they started whispering questions for me to ask, one on top of the other. I kept my pace slow so I wouldn't get caught, but I let my ghost answer as many questions as he could, as quick as he could.

He was seventeen when he died, he drowned in Lake Chicot, and it was cold on the other side. The only question

I didn't let my ghost answer was his name, because I couldn't think of one outside of people we already knew.

It took forever to spell everything out, and even though it was fun yanking Ben's and Collette's chains, I was hot and getting tired from controlling all my tiny sneak pushes.

The last thing I spelled out was *over the river*, to answer Ben's question about where my ghost used to live. We had so many rivers in Ascension Parish that anybody could say they lived over one.

While Collette tried to puzzle out which river, I nudged the pointer toward ADDIO, saying goodbye so we could put the witchboard away.

It pained me to think about it being folded up and put back in its box; it was so pretty to look at that I'd have kept it out on a coffee table for people to admire.

"I wish we knew his name," Collette said.

The pointer veered before I got it to ADDIO, and my mouth went dry. Stealing looks at Ben's wrists, I could tell he wasn't pushing it, and my body went numb when I realized Collette wasn't, either. Their hands lay still as a pond, but I could feel the pull as the pointer swirled around the board.

Collette called the letters out, but I knew what it was before she finished. A tight band knotted around my heart, squeezing it painfully as I mouthed the name with no voice at all.

"Elijah."

Cold just like yesterday's came over me, icy seeds taking root and growing beneath my skin. Considering how hot it was, it should have felt good, but it ached instead. That was the name I would have picked—his was the only Incident we had. Maybe that fine board could read my mind; maybe I never needed to push.

The pointer slipped back and forth across the fine, polished wood, almost too fast to read, then skidded to a stop on ADDIO after finishing one whole sentence.

All three of us stared in silence at the message. It seemed too simple, too plain, to give us the chill it did.

Where y'at, Iris?

&

I ditched Collette and Ben at the Red Stripe and took the scenic route home. They planned to drain Lake Chicot with buckets if they had to; I didn't have the courage to tell them I'd made that part up. I didn't tell them about my book moving, either.

Elijah wanted to talk to *me*, which made it nice and even. Collette got dumb old Ben Duvall.

I wandered the edge of the road, picking butterfly weed to weave into a scarlet crown. The Incident was a haunt to me, a black fairy tale that went like this:

Once upon a time in the '80s, Elijah Landry went to bed, and when his mama came to wake him the next day, she found an empty room and a blood-dotted pillow instead. They searched all of Ascension Parish, but nobody ever saw him again, and only God or the devil knows what became of him. Amen.

We still had echoes of him, though. His mama decided that God had carried Elijah to heaven, body and all. She bought prayers on the church steps, a hard candy for a lit candle—the end of times was coming, she was sure.

27

And now that he'd spoken to me, I wanted more. I could've made up stories about him if I'd wanted to. Elijah could have been perfect or awful, beautiful or ugly, artistic or athletic, but I wanted to know the truth. Was he friendly? Did he like playing practical jokes? Was his hair dark? Were his eyes darker? He'd been real once; someone had to know the answers.

It didn't seem right to pester Old Mrs. Landry with questions. In her soft, sad mind, her boy was a saint, and I didn't think I could bring myself to shake her out of that.

Miles Took at the barbershop told some of the finest yarns around, but he was practically famous for what we politely called "exaggerating."

Down at the church, Father Rey told nothing but the gospel and the truth, but he hadn't lived here long enough to know Elijah. Collette's mama would ask too many questions about why I wanted to know and she'd tell Collette besides. Mr. Ourso at the Red Stripe hated everybody under thirty.

That left Daddy or the Internet, and as I crowned myself with crimson flowers, I decided it would be the latter. Daddy was plenty old enough to have known Elijah, but I didn't figure he'd care much for me digging around in old graves. He liked to look forward, not back.

Finally home, I closed the front door quietly to keep from waking Daddy. I toed off my sandals and flopped onto the couch in our front living room. The sofa was a wedding present from Mama's people, light blue and probably silk; it had delicate designs all over it and looked brand-new.

That, and a nameplate on a mausoleum, was all I had of her. Maybe other people kept mementos, but not my daddy.

Besides the sofa, my mama's things were gone, and according to Daddy, the sofa was too fine for sitting.

Which may have been true, but it was the coolest spot in the house. If I wasn't really supposed to sit there, wouldn't Daddy have put it somewhere besides right under the air conditioner?

I thought so and settled in.

chapter four

&

The air had a funny feel to it, heavier than it was supposed to be, hotter than usual. July got stingy with the wind, and even the birds and bugs kept their songs to themselves.

"We could ask Poseidon to raise him up," Collette said. Her breath puffed between words as we rode our bikes out to Lake Chicot.

I said, "Maybe there's nothing left down there."

Ben stood on his pedals as he coasted down the hill. "We shouldn't mess with other people's gods, I don't think."

"All right," Collette said. "We'll ask the naiads instead."

I didn't bother pointing out that the naiads were a river god's daughters. Why bother? They didn't need me to have a conversation, so I pretended I was mute.

Ben said, "I think we'll find something this time."

"I bet we do," Collette agreed.

Reaching the pier, Ben jumped off his bike and offered

Collette a hand down. I managed to make it to the shore on my own.

"The cattails are thick here," Collette said. She brushed her hand along the stalks, making their heavy heads bow before her. "Wonder if they fed on his body?"

Ben trailed Collette's touch with his fingers. "You want me to write that down as evidence?"

"If you would, please," she murmured.

I peeled off my sandals and sloshed ahead, breathing through quicksand. My chest was full of silt and stone, so I walked quicker. They didn't need me around for *that*, either, any more than I wanted to be.

Clinging to the truth of my haunt in the graveyard, I figured I'd let them have my pushed-around lies. My Elijah, my real one, was my secret.

At the edge of the lake, the water didn't bother moving. When I stepped in, warm algae laced around my ankles. Out toward the middle, it would be deeper and clearer, good to swim in, but I didn't want to walk home wet.

Voices drew me down the shore. I waved when I saw a couple of girls from our class sunning on the banks. Nikki lived down in the trailers, and Carrie Anne lived right inside the bayou. She was a champion frog gigger, even better than the boys. One time, she caught two on her spear at once.

"Hey, y'all," I said.

Carrie Anne shaded her eyes with her magazine. "Hey, Iris, what's up?"

"Nothing. Hot, ain't it?"

"I know, right?" Nikki sat up. "You going in?"

Sliding my hands into my back pockets, I shook my head. "Nah, just walking with Collette and Ben."

"Collette's here?" Nikki flew to her feet, looking past me to Collette "Oh snap, come here!"

Now, maybe I couldn't hold Collette's attention lately, but a good talk about French braiding and who knew the fancy twists could. I backed off, sort of embroidering the space around them until I ran into Ben.

"I don't think they're talking English anymore," he said. He pulled out a silver pocketknife and started peeling a switch. Strips of bark came off, baring pale, green wood beneath.

I shrugged. "I could translate."

"That's all right."

I flopped down in the dry, stingy grass. Without looking up, I asked, "You going out for baseball this summer?"

Ben streaked his knife down the switch. "Nah."

"How come?"

"Shea's better than me, and the scouts didn't come to see him, so . . ." He trailed off, shrugging.

I sat beside him. "You got time, though."

Turning his knife, he pressed the flat of the blade against his lower lip. His gaze turned toward the distance, watching gold spark off the waves. "I don't know if you know, but my mama's real sick."

I didn't want to, but I felt bad for him. "I know. I'm sorry."

"So it's probably better if I ain't going away to games, just in case."

Twisting a wood shaving around my finger, I nodded. "Probably."

Ben folded his knife and leaned forward, dangling it

between his knees. He looked tired. All at once, like he'd gathered up shadows to wrap himself in, he blurted out, "What do you do when your mama dies, Iris?"

"I don't know."

"Thanks," Ben said, quietly aggravated.

"I ain't messing with you, Ben. I don't remember having one. How could that be the same?"

That satisfied him, I guess, because he settled. "You ever try to call her up?"

"No." I said it hard and fast. "I wouldn't, ever."

Maybe I didn't remember her, but she wasn't old bones to me. She was human and sacred and real.

"I wouldn't either," Ben said, and I sighed. That meant we had something in common.

&

It took the breath out of me when Collette pulled out the chair at her own desk to let Ben sit in front of *her* computer. She leaned against the corner of the chair, swaying, playing with her hair as she leaned over his shoulder.

"Where're you gonna look?" she asked, like she hadn't ever seen the Internet before.

Sitting on the edge of the bed, way out in Siberia, I watched Collette "accidentally" rub her arm against Ben's as he typed. He incidentally grazed his cheek against her hair when he turned to talk to her. Huddled together, they blocked the screen so I couldn't see, and I sort of expected I wasn't meant to.

"I'm not finding anything," Ben said.

Collette reached over his shoulder, typing with one finger. "Okay, hit ENTER."

Rubbing my thumb into my palm, I considered my escape. It would be too obvious to jump out the window, and I'd have to bump all around them to get out the door. I thought if I wished hard enough, I could just astral-project and go home. My spirit, at least—my body could wait till supper to come home.

"Here's an Elijah Landry."

I jerked my head up, but I still couldn't see the screen. "What did you find?"

Collette didn't look back. "It's not him; don't worry about it."

"This says there are five people in the whole country with his same name."

I tried again. "But is he our one?"

Ben said, "Nah," and went back to typing. They didn't say anything else. They clicked and clicked, shuffling through Web sites and leaving me on hold.

The window looked better all the time, and I wondered if I'd get to eat nothing but ice cream if I ended up in the hospital with a broken leg.

"It seems like there should be something," Ben complained.

"You'd think," Collette said.

"You wanna go back to the lake?"

All off balance, I needed the ground to feel solid under my feet again, so I interrupted. I didn't look directly at them, but I did raise my voice enough to be heard.

"If we can get a ride to St. Amant, I know a better place to look."

Mrs. Lanoux looked like Collette, only older, her lines starker and sharper. She kept her hair up, twisted and held fast in a silver wire cage. A few curls escaped, framing her sweet tea-shaded cheeks.

She left a half-moon ring of cranberry lipstick on her glass when she put it down, pointing at us with a yardstick when we came in. "Unless you're here to work, you can turn right back around."

No fool, Ben backed onto the sidewalk. I stayed at the door, but Collette, unafraid, walked up to the counter. "Can you put the sign out and take us to the library?"

"I'm running a business here," Mrs. Lanoux said, then suddenly whipped her head around. "Rooster, if you don't quit playing in my purse, so help me . . ."

Turning her mother's glass, Collette stole a drink from the unmarked side, then put it back quick before she got caught. "Nobody's coming in till lunch. You have time."

"What do you want to go to the library for, anyway?"

Collette shrugged. "Look at some books."

Mrs. Lanoux crossed her arms on the counter and leaned forward. "You've got a whole room full of books at home."

"It's the fifteenth," I said helpfully. I offered a bright smile and a wave when Mrs. Lanoux turned her attention to me. "They get their new books on the fifteenth."

Catching the scent of a liar, Mrs. Lanoux arched one thin brow at me. "Is that so?"

I kept my smile going. "That's what my daddy says."

With a stretch, Mrs. Lanoux straightened again. "Look now. Y'all want a little, you gotta give a little. I have grease traps that need cleaning and a Rooster that needs minding."

Collette melted against the counter, groaning. "Mama, come on!"

"How about it, darlin'?" Mrs. Lanoux disappeared behind the pie case, coming back up with her purse in one hand and a handful of Rooster's collar in the other. She carried on with her thought even as she hustled Collette's squirming brother from behind the counter. "I could make you work every day, like Patsy does Lonette at the gas station."

A hand fell on my shoulder and I jumped, startled. Wound up tight, I slowly looked over my shoulder, expecting brown eyes and a laughing *Where you at?* but it was just Ben.

"Tell her to never mind. My brother's gonna take us. Come on," he whispered.

Before I could answer, he bolted off. Left to make up an excuse, I scratched a mosquito bite on my ankle and said, "Collette. Collette!"

She rolled her eyes and her body, twisting around to face me. "What?"

Using all my psychic powers and a good, strong bug-eyed look, I commanded her to play along. "We can go later. I just saw the mail truck, and Uncle Lee said he was sending me some catalogs. You wanna go see if they're here?"

Collette stared blankly for two seconds, then kick-started. "Oh, those candy ones?"

"It better be candy ones," Mrs. Lanoux said, turning a place mat over and slapping down some crayons for Rooster to draw with.

Me and Collette had both learned the meaning of the

word *confiscated* when Mrs. Lanoux caught us with one of Uncle Lee's novelty catalogs. She didn't think farting piggy banks were too awful funny.

I backed against the door to open it. "They are, swear."

Mrs. Lanoux waved us off with her yardstick.

As she passed me, Collette said, "Nice save. Now what?"

***

Cars never died in Ondine; they just got handed down. Shea Duvall's ancient station wagon wasn't pretty or quiet, but it ran, and that was all that mattered.

For two dollars each, Shea volunteered to ferry us two towns over to the library, and for one dollar more, he didn't even ask us why we wanted to go. He didn't care; he just wanted the extra dollar.

"I'm not made of money," Collette huffed as she handed the hush money over the backseat.

I settled in against plastic seats that had gone soft in the sun and radiated an oily perfume. The engine droned so loud we couldn't hear ourselves talk. The sound of it echoed in my ears, even after Shea had dumped us in front of the library.

The librarian stopped shuffling magazines when we walked in. Drifting back toward her desk, she looked suspicious, or maybe curious—like she knew we had other places to be in the middle of the summer, so why weren't we in them? By the time we got to her, though, she just seemed professional again.

"We want to look at newspapers," I said when she asked if she could help us. "Old ones."

She picked up a pen and scrawled a note. Offering it to me between two fingers, she said, "Take that to West; he's shelving in the back."

Waiting until we got out of her line of sight, I turned the note over and read it to Collette and Ben. "Microfiche, June through July, 1989."

"How did she know?" Collette asked softly.

I answered with a shrug, leading her and Ben like I knew where I was going. Straight back, and then we rounded the corner to find one of the juniors from St. Amant reading against a library cart.

His plastic name tag said WEST—VOLUNTEER—I CAN HELP! but with his hair in his face, he didn't even see us until Collette dipped down and waved at him.

"The librarian told us to find you," I said, and gave him the note.

He read it, then shoved it in his pocket. Jerking his head to get us to follow, he kept stealing glances back at Collette. "Y'all looking for Elijah Landry?"

Collette smiled. "How did you know?"

I exchanged a quick look with Ben; I almost felt sorry for him. He had this pinched look, and I think he woulda said something if West hadn't lifted a box from a file cabinet and handed it to him.

"It's either old people doing their family tree," West said, handing me a box, "or people who think they're gonna solve a mystery nobody else did. Y'all ain't old."

"Old enough," Collette said.

Ben shook his box. "How does this stuff work, anyway?"

I'd expected to spend an afternoon sweltering in some

back room, wheezing over old, yellow newspapers. Microfiche turned out to be movies, sort of.

West threaded one of the spools into the machine and flipped on a light. He turned the knob, and like a miracle, a whole newspaper page jumped onto the screen.

"You take care," West said when I turned the knob too hard. "I have to tape 'em if you break 'em."

Collette shot me a funny look, but I promised we'd be careful. West lingered behind Collette's chair another minute, until Ben made a specific point of thanking him for his help.

Once West was out of earshot, Collette leaned over to whisper, "He was nice."

"I guess," Ben said coolly.

I minded my own business. Old pages from the *Ascension Citizen* flashed by in gray streaks. My eyes flitted back and forth, trying to make sense of the blurs, until a headache started between my brows. Slowing the wheel, I found I could actually skim the headlines.

Eighteen-year-old baseball scores, wedding announcements, obituaries; the parish president looking for money to repave the roads . . . That one was kind of funny, because Daddy still complained about the roads and how somebody ought to do something about them.

Collette had just gotten her machine running when I stopped half on a back page, half on a front. I turned the wheel as slow as I could, evening the picture up, then reached over to tug on Collette's sleeve. "Look, June seventeenth."

Craning over my shoulder, Collette read the article out loud with me. " 'Landry, seventeen, had just been released from Ascension Parish Hospital when he disappeared.' " Collette pushed ringlets out of her face to look at me. "It doesn't say why he was there, though."

Nodding, I skimmed farther down, past the quotes from his teachers that said he was a good student and a nice boy. " 'A spokesman for the sheriff's department said they found no evidence of forced entry during their initial investigation.' "

"How 'bout that," Collette said, laying her forearm against my shoulders to get more comfortable. "Look, right there. 'Mr. Nathan Landry and his wife, Babette, are offering a twenty-thousand-dollar reward.' Did y'all know there was a Mr. Landry?"

"I guess there had to be," I said slowly. "I never thought about it, though."

Ben slid into Collette's empty chair. "I knew."

"How come you didn't say anything?" Collette asked.

"I dunno." Ben shrugged, his shoulders swimming in his oversized T-shirt. "A couple years after Elijah disappeared, they split up. 'Bout the time Old Mrs. Landry decided God called Elijah home, my mama said."

Collette shooed Ben from her chair. "What else do you know that we don't?"

Ben laughed. "How am I supposed to know what you know?"

Hiding a smile behind my hand, I tried not to look overlong at Ben in case I started liking him a little. I didn't want to hold his hand or anything. He was Collette's; I wouldn't like him like that. But when she wasn't wallowing all over him, he *did* make me laugh.

I cleared my throat. "We're supposed to be reading, not talking."

Collette muttered something under her breath but got back to work. The clack and chunk of spools winding started to take on a pattern, regular as a train on its tracks. Adding my part to it, I turned the wheel slowly, getting used to the swipes of gray that turned steady black-and-white when I stopped to read.

"Says here he was on the football team." Ben waggled his finger at the screen.

"My daddy was on the team," I said.

"Think he'd tell us anything?"

I shrugged, as if I hadn't already considered it. "I dunno."

Making her machine whine with a particularly hard crank, Collette sniffed like she'd smelled something bad. "He works the night shift, anyhow. We'd have to be up at dawn or midnight to have a sit-down with him."

"Not on the weekends." I cut her a look for answering for me. "I'll ask at dinner." Then I pointed to my screen. "A whole mess of people went looking for him; half the parish, it sounds like."

Collette took the pen and paper from Ben. "Well, we knew that. Did they quote anybody?"

In all, we made a list of six names, mostly folks who'd worked on the search parties, a couple people who'd claimed to be his friends. By the time we'd run out of microfiche, we had pages of clues, some in Ben's scratchy print, others in Collette's fat, round cursive.

Collette and I packed the films away, making sure they got back in the right cases. It didn't seem right that a whole mystery, a whole summer, could fit in such a small space. The spools clattered when I carried the box to Ben, who was finishing up on his machine.

Nose almost pressed against the screen, Ben murmured and pointed to a picture he'd found. " 'S Elijah, look."

Most of the articles had used a yearbook picture about the size of a stamp, too fuzzy to really make anything out. This one took up a quarter of the front page, and it made the back of my neck prickle.

In fuzzy, faded color, Elijah peeked up through a fringe of ruffled bangs. He had dark hair, dark eyes, and a smiling mouth I could practically see curving to ask me where I was at.

"That's him," I said. "That's who I saw." I saw the spark in the cemetery again, heard his voice coming back so clear he could have been standing right behind me. For a second, I thought he might be, that his hand would curl around my shoulder, cold and steady, to lead me to his last, lonely place on earth.

When Collette bumped me to get a look, I jumped.

"You sure, Iris?"

Nodding, I wrapped my arms around myself, rubbing to try to get a taste of the heat I'd been glad to escape all day. We were looking for Elijah because I had lied, but there he was—my boy from the cemetery—and I didn't know if that was coincidence or destiny or what, but it sure felt like somebody'd walked over my grave.

I couldn't stop staring; by the time Ben and Collette figured out how to get a print, I'd memorized Elijah's face, down to the crook in his nose and the spray of freckles on his cheeks.

Even if I'd only imagined my visions, even if we'd all told a lie on the witchboard, I knew when I saw that picture that Elijah wanted me to find him.

In my heart, I knew he was ready to come home.

℘

Back at my house, I found a note on the fridge. They'd called Daddy in early to work, and my supper was waiting for me in the oven. A quick peek inside revealed a meat loaf, which meant I would cut off a slice to feed to the garbage disposal, then microwave a frozen pizza.

Meandering around the kitchen, I wrapped myself in an eerie calm. The first time me and Collette tried talking to the dead, somebody answered. My thoughts had been twisted up in knots. One minute, everything going on was true; the next, it wasn't. Collette could talk me into believing something, but then I'd turn around and let Daddy talk me right back out.

I'd stumbled back and forth so much, it was a relief to finally be sure about something.

Elijah chose me. He'd chosen *me*. Collette had lain three feet away, working the same spell, but Elijah had said *my* name. *I'd* seen him; no one else had. Plenty of other people wanted to know what had happened to him; one of them in particular would be on the church steps come Sunday morning, offering hard candy for prayers.

But he chose *me*.

43

chapter five

&

The day started hazy gray, threatening rain right from the beginning. When I opened my window, the sticky green smell of it rolled in on a warm breeze. The curtains fluttered, blowing out and rippling at the edges, whispering against my desk.

I hurried to get dressed and start investigating. Me and Collette and Ben had split our list of people quoted in the paper on the subject of Elijah, and Deputy Wood was on mine. The sheriff's station was right outside town, close enough that I could ride my bike.

In old pictures, Deputy Wood had stood tall and skinny, with a thick black mustache that waterfalled down either side of his mouth. Having seen him lately, though, I knew that his mustache had gone salt-and-pepper and he'd thickened out in the middle. The blue uniform stretched tight across his chest, and his star didn't lie flat anymore.

Most days, he sat in his cruiser just off the highway, cherry-picking the hot-rodders who had nothing to do but drive fast between Ondine and Baton Rouge. Everybody over sixteen hated him, but since I couldn't drive yet, he seemed all right to me. Besides, I thought folks ought to know better than to speed on his stretch, anyway. Gambling on its being his day off came with pretty bad odds.

I wasn't sure if it was against the law to walk up to him while he was working, but I figured the worst that could happen was that he'd send me home with a warning to stay off the big roads. Since I'd be on my bike, he wouldn't clock me at more than five miles an hour, so I couldn't get a ticket; I just might be wasting my morning.

On my way out, I stopped at the Red Stripe to get a soda. Fishing around for the coldest can, I leaned into the refrigerator case and apologized when Mr. Ourso shuffled past with a box of toilet paper nearly bigger than him.

I felt like I should help him. I knew better than to offer, though, because he liked things just so. Even Ben just opened and unpacked the boxes when he worked; he left everything in the back for Mr. Ourso to put away. Mr. Ourso was particular about everything in the Red Stripe, probably because that was all he had.

Normally, I wouldn't have given him much thought, but his name was on our list, too. He hadn't joined the search parties—my guess was he'd been old even then—but he had donated sandwiches and coffee. Since everybody had met up here, he'd have to know something, even if it was just the places they'd looked and found nothing.

When I got to the register, I was careful to hold my can instead of setting it down. I didn't want to get a dirty look for leaving a ring on his counter. Mr. Ourso returned from the back, scrubbed his hands with a dish towel, then threw it over his shoulder when he saw me waiting.

"Got some salt and vinegar chips that go real good with that," he said, nodding at my soda as he opened the gate to get behind the counter. "They're on sale."

I hesitated, because I didn't really like salt and vinegar chips. They were only fifty cents, though, and I thought Mr. Ourso might like me a little better if I bought them. Plucking a green bag from the stand, I turned and dropped it on the counter with a smile. "Now I'm set."

Nodding, Mr. Ourso punched a couple of buttons on his register, one at a time. He probably knew how much everything in the Red Stripe cost, down to the penny and the tax, but he always rang it up slowly anyway.

Since I had him there, I didn't see anything wrong with asking about Elijah. I did just buy a snack from him I didn't want after all. "Hey, Mr. Ourso?"

He answered me with a grunt, the register chiming when he hit TOTAL. "Two sixty-two."

I dug the last of my coins from my pocket. Between Shea and Mr. Ourso, finding Elijah had started to get expensive. "You've had the Red Stripe a long time, huh?"

"Forty-seven years," he said. He smoothed my dollars with the heel of his hand before putting them in the register. I guess he didn't want the rest of the money getting any ideas about being unruly in the drawer.

"Wow."

He looked up at me with watery blue eyes, but he didn't nod, or smile, or even frown. He had the stillest face I'd ever seen. Thin lines dug down around his mouth and across his brow, but he seemed made out of paper. I could see the thin blue veins beneath his skin. In fact, I could see his heartbeat, his pulse fluttering at his temple. The quiet scared me more than yelling would have, and I think I might have flinched when he said, "Thirty-eight cents."

The change went in my pocket, and I mumbled a thank-you as I slunk toward the door. Tucking the chips and soda into my bike bag, I decided that cracking Mr. Ourso could wait until later. A lot later.

&

Sweaty and out of breath, I stood on the side of the high-way. There were tire tracks where Deputy Wood should have been; he must have needed some new scenery.

In my brilliant plans, he was sitting right out in his cherry-picking spot, just waiting to spill terrible secrets about Elijah's disappearance, if only somebody would come along and ask him.

I stood there for a long time, like wishing would make his cruiser appear. Funny enough, it didn't, so I got back on my bike.

The police outpost wasn't much, just a cinder-block box with some dingy windows, but it had air-conditioning, at least. The frigid, tinny blast of it went right through my sweat-soaked shirt as I approached the front desk.

The woman there didn't look up from her computer. Her fingers rushed along, still going as she asked, "Can I help you?"

"I'm looking for Deputy Wood," I said. I craned to see if he might be in the back. "Is he here?"

"He's on patrol. Is there something I can help you with?"

"I don't know," I said, studying her smooth skin and unlined hands. "How old are you?"

The typing stopped. "Excuse me?"

Something started bubbling in my chest. "I mean, I was wondering about something that happened a long time ago, and you don't look very old. . . ."

The woman typed out four more letters, pounding the keyboard hard on each one before spinning her chair to face me. "Do you have a report number?"

I shook my head. "No, ma'am."

"Do you have new evidence you'd like to share?"

"No, ma'am."

"Are you an interested party?"

Drawing my shoulders up, I hesitated. "Well, I *am* interested."

Her voice clipped, she plucked a pen out of a can on her desk and produced a form. "If there's something you want to claim, fill out your name and address, and to the best of your abilities, describe the object or objects you believe should be returned to you."

I shook my head when she tried to hand me the pen. "There's nothing I want, not a *thing* I want, I mean. I just wanted to talk to Deputy Wood."

She whisked the form off the counter and replaced it with a new one. "Requests for interviews need to go through the Public Information Office."

"I don't want to interview him. I just want to talk to him!"

The woman drew her fingers across the counter. She spoke slowly, like I wasn't bright enough to follow her. "About a police matter?"

"No, ma'am, never mind," I said, and gave up.

Waterlogged and weepy, I got back on my bike. Between jerking my head back every time I snuffled and trying to swipe at my face to keep my view clear, it was a lucky thing I didn't get run over.

More than anything, I just wanted to be home, curled up in the armchair, rubbing my fingers on the air conditioner. I wanted to be home just like that, right that minute, but I was stuck.

Daddy didn't keep the ringer on in his room during the daytime, so even if I'd had a way to call, he wouldn't have answered. Collette's mama would have come to fetch me, but I could imagine the way her voice would go up and down all the way home if she had to leave the diner to carry me home.

The highway was dizzy hot, white waves rolling off the asphalt to make fun-house mirages out of the distance. I kept telling myself I only had to make it to the next sign, but the next sign always looked closer than it was.

Cars zipped by me, and sometimes, out of pure mean-ness, they honked. It was a surprise every time, and I kept wobbling off into the gravel to get away from them.

I wished horrible things on those people. I prayed they'd get a flat tire and have to walk—at least I had a bicycle. And then, when I ran across them staggering toward Ondine, I'd laugh and pedal faster.

Meanness of spirit was all I had left in me. I was burning from the inside, my legs started turning to jelly, and it got harder to keep myself from sitting down in the tall grass to bawl.

I hated that woman at the sheriff's station, her and her

dyed red hair that wasn't fooling anybody; I hated Deputy Wood for being somewhere besides his cherry-picking spot, where he could have written slips for half of Ascension Parish, considering how fast everybody drove past me.

Just for good measure, I hated Shea Duvall, too, because he didn't happen past on a whim and pick me up. Me and my bike would have fit in the back of his bronze and primer station wagon just fine, and I had almost a dollar left. That should have been enough for a ride home. Next time I saw him, I planned to call him Horatio, just out of spite—he'd been named for a Shakespeare character, too.

The sky folded over on itself, new shades of bruise and brown painting the clouds, but the rain wouldn't come, no matter how hard I wished it. Road dirt clung to my sweaty skin, and my clothes were soaked through. A good gully washer would clean me off and cool me down, and besides, nobody would be able to tell I had cried all the way home if the rain came.

I slid off my bike to walk it for a while; as I walked I made mystic signs with one hand, like I was one of those traveling rainmakers who used to come through during a drought. I kept at it until the sky finally opened.

Whether I had anything to do with it or not, I took credit for the storm. Maybe the secret to making wonders happen was just waiting for the right time to try.

&

I left my bike in the front yard, and I'd just started inside when I saw the red and blue lights coming down my street, gliding slow enough that I knew the police weren't on an emergency.

The rain dulled everything, even the bright red stripes on the white-paneled sheriff's car, and it made the tires sound like they had a scrub brush to the pavement.

My heart jumped, beating hard and happy in my chest. Elijah had decided to help after all, sending Deputy Wood all but to my door. I squeezed the wet from the hem of my shirt, as if that'd make me more presentable, and waited.

Rennie Delancie came onto his porch with a big aw-shucks smile. His strawberry-blond hair fell into his eyes, and I guessed if you liked the wicked type, Rennie was probably pretty fine to look at. Waving a bandaged hand at me he shifted from one foot to the other, looking like he had to pee.

Since gawking was rude, I pretended to fumble for my key, listening as Deputy Wood went up Rennie's walk.

"No, sir, we haven't blown up anything for weeks."

Rennie lied like most people breathed, natural and smooth. I couldn't see him, but I figured he had painted on that smile of his until it was permanent.

Rennie and Deputy Wood went back and forth awhile; the bandage came from a cooking accident, and Lord, no, he hadn't heard anything out of the ordinary. Deputy Wood took a peek in the garage and around the back of the house, then told Rennie he and his brother needed to knock it off or next time he'd haul them in. They probably heard that once a week, though, so when Rennie said, "Yes, sir, I promise," I laughed under my breath.

Deputy Wood headed for his car, and I jumped down the steps. I tried to walk fast but not too fast, in case that was suspicious, and caught him as he fit himself behind the steering wheel again.

"Everything all right, sugar?" He hung his hat out the door, shaking the rain off before tossing it onto the seat next to him.

"Yes, sir, but could I ask you a question?"

Deputy Wood turned down the radio on his shoulder. He rested an arm across the steering wheel and grinned up at me. His dark brown eyes sparkled. They didn't look as old as the rest of him did. "Besides that one?"

"Yes, sir." I blushed, but I didn't shy away. "You helped look for Elijah Landry, didn't you?"

"Well, me and most of the parish, but yes, ma'am, I did." His smile curled with curiosity, crooked at one corner like his brows. "I reckon that was before your time, though."

I nodded. "It was, but I was . . . Me and my friend, we're gonna do a report on local mysteries, and that's the biggest one we've got."

"I don't know that it's much of a mystery," he said. "Fact is, he probably run off."

I didn't mean to shake my head, but I did. Folks ran away from Ondine all the time; it was practically tradition. When you lived in a town as big as a flea, anywhere with a movie theater was a step up. Everybody in town had an uncle or cousin what did that and nobody ever searched for them except maybe their mamas.

So right off, Elijah's disappearance was different.

"How come you all had that big search party?"

Grinning again, Deputy Wood crooked a finger to draw me closer, then whispered like he was telling a secret. "His granddaddy was friends with the parish president."

What that had to do with anything, I wasn't sure, but I didn't say that. "There was blood on his pillow, too."

"Sugar, if you've ever had a nosebleed, there's probably been blood on your pillow." Deputy Wood had finished answering questions. Twisting himself to sit proper in the car, he reached up to play with his radio. "How about you write your report on fox fire? I had some follow me half a mile once. Now, that's a mystery."

Disappointed, I shook my head. "My daddy says that's just swamp gas lighting up." I shrugged and stepped up on the curb, curling a hand against my forehead to keep the rain from my eyes.

&

For me and Daddy, talking didn't stop at the end of supper, but the subjects changed. Dinner-table conversation covered news and information; dish-washing talk was sort of philosophical, or maybe just thinking out loud, so it was the best time to bring up Elijah.

"Deputy Wood says Elijah Landry just run off."

Daddy hummed, the sound lost in plate clatter. "Does he, now?"

"Yup." Digging into the corner of a pan, I scraped hard to get the last of the cheese off. "He said the only reason folks looked for him was because of his granddaddy's friends."

"Well, Mark Wood never did think too hard or too long." Taking the pan, Daddy glanced at me. "That's between us; you respect your elders."

Crossing my heart, I nodded. "Anyway, so what's that

got to do with it? If somebody took me, people would look, right? Even though we don't know the parish president?"

Without hesitating, Daddy took the next plate with a nod. "Naturally, sugar, but you're younger than Elijah was. And a girl."

Daddy usually made things more clear, but with that, he had jumped in with Deputy Wood to complicate things. My questions weren't hard—"What?" and "Why?" mostly—so there ought to have been simple answers. "So?"

"Elijah was just shy of being grown. It's not against the law to be grown and leave if you want." Daddy turned the faucet to his side of the sink, rerinsing glasses before putting them in the tray. "Folks don't worry about boys as much. It may not be right, but that's the way it is."

"Well, what do you think?"

Putting a glass down hard, Daddy chimed it against the rest of them, the whole drainer rattling. Tension tightened his mouth to a thin line. "I think he's gone, Iris, and that's the most anybody can say."

I swallowed, feeling vaguely ashamed, though I didn't know why. "I'm sorry."

As if he'd remembered something, Daddy shook his head, and the lines drawn around his mouth faded. "What's got you thinking about it, anyway?"

"I just wondered." Then I added, "You knew him, right?"

Daddy flipped his towel over. "It's a small town; everybody did."

"But he was in your class."

Stopping for a minute, Daddy turned to me. "What are you after?"

54

Shrugging, I swiped a plate with my sponge and passed it to him. I couldn't answer that honestly, partly because it was a secret and partly because I didn't want him to warn me off of it. "I don't know."

Leaving the dish in the sink, Daddy scrubbed his hand dry and put it on my shoulder. "Are you afraid of staying here at night by yourself? Baby, if you are, Mrs. Thacker—"

"No!"

Mrs. Thacker was seventysomething, and she smelled like a house full of cats. Until last fall, Daddy had paid her to come in at night to keep an eye on me. Being a widow herself, Mrs. Thacker grieved for my daddy and for my mama in a way that made me feel sick to my stomach. Her chandelier earrings rang like church bells calling good people to Mass, sending good people to God. She was forever prodding me to talk about Mama so I wouldn't forget. I hated Mrs. Thacker's knobby knuckles and her morbid chiming, but I knew it wasn't polite to ignore your elders, so I made things up to make her leave me alone.

A visit to Mississippi for a cousin's funeral had kept Mrs. Thacker away for a week last September, and I'd used that week to convince Daddy she was completely unnecessary.

"I'm fine on my own, I promise."

The quiet went on and on while Daddy thought about it; then he nodded. "All right, then, if you're sure."

"I am." In my head, I added, *One hundred percent, absolutely, totally sure,* but I kept that to myself. If I sounded too eager, it might make him suspicious.

Returning to my dishes, I twisted the tap to add more hot water to my side. Carefully, I wound my way toward the right subject again. "Anyway, I was just curious because me and Collette read some stories about him at the library. They said he was on the football team."

Daddy held his hand out for another plate. "He kept track of the equipment."

That little sentence seemed to sparkle; it was so real, like a direct line to Elijah. "He couldn't play, then?"

"No, he could." A faraway gaze settled over Daddy. "He volunteered to be the manager since his mama wouldn't sign his permission slip."

Before I could ask why not, Daddy put the last plate in the drainer and changed the subject. "How'd you run up on Deputy Wood, anyhow?"

Lucky for me, I could tell the truth. I don't know what I would have said if I'd found him on the highway, after all.

&

My bedroom ceiling had plaster swirls on it, and when I couldn't sleep, I liked to stare at it and try to make new patterns out of the curls. I followed the shadows with my gaze, waves hitting the trim and flowing back into fancy swirls. Curlicues drifted into ribbons, splaying into butterflies. They flew away over green, green grass, leading me to the creek.

The scent of rich, dark earth tickled my nose, and I pushed tallgrass aside to get to the water. My heart turned over when I finally reached the riverbank. Lying there propped on one elbow, chucking rocks into the water, was Elijah.

Scooping up another stone, he drew back lazily, measuring his mark with his eyes before he threw. Somehow I'd expected him to be skinny like Ben, but he wasn't. He had a fine shape, with broad shoulders and strong arms.

My shadow fell on him, and he tipped his baseball hat back to look up at me. I'd been right; he had dark brown eyes to go with his brown hair, and creamy, Acadian skin with a hint of peach to it.

Smiling crookedly, he flicked his rock toward the water. "Where y'at, Iris?"

Swimming awake, I blinked at my desk and my posters. Dark as ever, my room didn't smell like anything, and I was alone, just like I should have been. Swinging my feet over the side of the bed, I stood up, unsteady because somehow I expected marshy earth under me instead of carpet.

I stumbled to my desk so I could write down the details of my dream. It started to unravel in my head as I yanked my spellbook from the drawer. Flipping past the warning curse and all our other incantations, I stopped on the last half-used page.

Leaning over the spellbook, I slashed the page with ink, my handwriting sloped long like afternoon shadows. My words spilled out. They crashed into each other, and I had to read over them to make sure they were sense and not scribbles.

I flipped through the book once more before I collapsed back in bed. Throwing my forearm across my eyes, I exhaled, waiting for sleep to creep up on me again.

Then, against the blackness of my eyelids, I saw tiny print letters, soft white on dark. They rose like a ghost, chilling me till the hair stood up on my arms.

It's a dream, I told myself. *You're just sleeping again.*

But I heard the crickets singing outside. My nightgown

stuck to my skin, and a sour taste bittered the back of my tongue. That was waking; I was awake.

Scrambling out of bed, I tore through my spellbook. I stopped and flattened my hand on the page, the one that had floated up behind my closed eyes. My throat went tight; I couldn't breathe.

Somebody had written in my book.

My sprawling cursive had been marked out. I didn't have a spell to go crazy anymore, not according to the new block letters at the top of the page.

I had a spell called *How to Talk to Elijah*.

chapter six

&

In Ondine, we were bred with God and superstition in our blood. If we spilled salt, we threw some over our shoulder right away. And we always found wood nearby to knock on when we were graced with good fortune.

That renamed spell was a sign if I'd ever seen one.

The morning after my dream, I went to the cemetery. I closed the gate and counted my paces to Cecily Claiborne's crypt. I couldn't do anything about the cloudless sky and the flood of sunshine. Hoping the weather wouldn't matter, I climbed onto Cecily's slab.

Just like before, I spread my arms in a cross. I licked my lips, then took a long, slow breath, willing the spell to take hold. This was the spell to talk to Elijah—he was coming, and I would be ready.

The cicadas ticked slowly, the heat too much for them to work very hard. Everything seemed to stop—no clouds moved across the sky, no wind teased the trees. I had nothing but quiet in a place of the dead.

Closing my eyes against the steady sun, I called Elijah to me, repeating his name over and over in my thoughts until the sound of it was a song. It carried and floated, turning and turning until it didn't mean anything anymore, and I got lost in it.

Elijah, Elijah, Elijah.

A hand fell on my shoulder, and I jolted up. Somehow, all the shadows in the graveyard had gotten rearranged, and it hurt when I moved.

Standing next to Cecily's crypt, Collette shook her head at me. "Lord, you're burned."

Automatically, I touched my cheek, then pulled my fingers away with a hiss. I had a sandpaper tongue, and my skin felt tight and hot, even when I didn't touch it.

"You better get some aloe," Collette said. I could tell from her thin frown that she couldn't figure out why I'd do something so stupid as take a nap in the cemetery.

I slid off the slab and winced when I landed. "I've got some."

Falling into step with me, Collette watched me from the corner of her eye. She thought that made her look witchy and powerful. "What were you doing, anyway?"

"Frog gigging. See my boat?" I said, irritated. She knew good and well what the cemetery was for; she didn't need to ask me stupid questions. "What are *you* doing here?"

"Looking for you, ya think?"

"Well, you found me, ya think?"

Collette lifted her hair from her neck to cool off and

rolled her eyes. "Well, if you don't want to know what I found out, fine."

"Who said I didn't?"

Because I did want to know. She had a list of names, too, and we were supposed to meet up after supper to share our research.

"You don't act like it." Raising her nose in the air, Collette put on her queen attitude; she didn't even need a crown to do it. It didn't last long, though. Her curls bounced and her eyes sparkled, the way they always did when she was fit to explode with something interesting. "Elijah didn't know how to swim. You know why?"

It took me a minute to answer, because I couldn't wrap my head around that. If she'd said Elijah only ate pickled eggs, it wouldn't have sounded as strange. If you lived in Ondine, you knew how to swim.

"His mama wouldn't let him." Collette nodded, her eyes gone round and amazed. "She didn't let him swim or wear shorts or play games where he'd have to touch somebody, because it was a sin!"

At first, I wanted to argue with her, because I'd seen Elijah in shorts. Just like I knew God was real, I knew that once upon a time, Elijah'd lain on the creek bank and chucked stones into the water.

Of course, I wasn't supposed to sit on my mama's couch and I did it anyhow, so Collette's information and mine could both be true.

"Who told you that?"

Collette grinned. "Miss Nan, down at the gas station. I asked Uncle Teddy about Elijah, and he said I should talk to her." Collette's grin spread, as she leaned in to whisper, "They were going out behind his mama's back."

"She told you that?"

"Yuh huh." Dancing around me, Collette yanked on my arm and pulled me along. "And she said if we wanted to know more, we could come down to her trailer anytime."

My sunburn kept me from bouncing, but I wanted to. We had a personal invitation for an interview with somebody who'd probably known Elijah better than almost anybody. "You wanna go now?"

"We should wait for Ben." Then she made a face at him in his absence. "That way we don't have to repeat ourselves."

I made a face, too. "He's wasting a whole day for us."

"I know!"

Dust rose under our feet as we scuffed away from the graveyard.

"You hungry?" she asked.

"Just for something sweet."

Collette's mama only made us sweep up to pay for our pie, so in spite of my sunburn, it was a mighty fine afternoon.

&

"I don't think my daddy wants to talk about it," I said, sitting on the Duvalls' back stoop.

Sunset colored the sky with purples and oranges, shades that flattered Collette as she leaned against the porch rail. "How come?"

" 'Cause he was all cagey when I brought it up."

Ben wandered the same two squares of sidewalk. Watching

62

the empty window instead of us, he thought out loud. "Maybe if one of us did?"

Piping in, Collette said, "Uh-uh, once her daddy decides something, it's decided. Besides, we got Miss Nan, and you haven't even done your list yet."

Looking toward the house again, Ben lowered his voice. "Mama says you can't believe anything that comes from Nan Burkett's mouth. She's easy."

I wrinkled my nose. "That doesn't make her a liar."

"That's just what she said."

Ben stuck his hands in his pockets. "I think we ought to try the witchboard again."

Collette jumped on that right away. "Oooh, we could ask him who to talk to."

"We've already got a list," I protested, afraid they would see my eyes and know I'd done most of the talking on the board last time.

"We'll still do the list. But we should do this, too." Collette's voice went up at the end, and I looked back at her, waiting for her next brilliant idea. "This time we should do it at night. The dead are closer at night."

"Why is that?" Ben didn't sound like he expected an answer; he was just filling up space until he thought of what he really wanted to say. "Nighttime's fine by me, except I have to be home by ten."

A shadow crossed Collette's brow. "How come? Shea comes into the diner almost till midnight sometimes."

"I have to count out Mama's pills," Ben said flatly.

She should have left it alone at that, but sometimes Collette didn't know when to quit. She tried to sound concerned, at least. "Shouldn't your daddy be doing that?"

63

His voice flat, Ben answered, "I do it."

I cut in, trying to save everybody. "Then we can't, because it should be at midnight."

"That's the witching hour," Collette agreed. Peeling herself off the rail, she bounded down to sit on the bottom step, next to my feet. She folded her hands on her knees and looked up at Ben, serious. "After you're done counting, sneak out."

Ben shook his head. "Dang, y'all, she's right there in the kitchen."

A little quieter, Collette pressed on. "Look, all you have to do is set your watch for a quarter till, then climb out your window. I'll take the witchboard home tonight so you don't have to carry it."

"What about Iris?"

Collette snorted. "Her dad works nights, remember? She can go anywhere she wants."

That wasn't exactly true. My daddy let me roam where I wanted during the day. After dark, though, when the purple sky started going black in the distance, I had to be at home with the doors locked.

Changing sides to help Ben, I said, "If I get caught out, I'll get switched."

"You haven't been switched ever," Collette said.

"Probably 'cause she never got caught out." Ben grinned, dropping his head so his sandy bangs fell in his eyes.

It was nice to see him smile after being so tense. He wasn't broad or fine like Elijah, but for an interloper, he wasn't too bad.

Scowling at both of us, Collette tried to shrug like she didn't care. "Then I'll just do it on my own."

"You'll get possessed," I said.

"Not without the board you won't," Ben said at the same time.

All of a sudden, the air tightened like guitar strings; I could almost hear the hum. People didn't make a habit of telling Collette no.

Locking my fingers together, I shut my mouth tight to keep from interrupting and just watched. If it had been me, Collette would have said something snappish and flounced on home, but I could see in the way she pursed her mouth that she was weighing her answer.

Then, very carefully and real slow, she said, "Well, I'd like to use yours since it's so nice, but if you don't want to lend it to me . . ."

"I don't. It was my nonna's."

A statue, that was what I tried to be, even though I wanted to laugh. I pressed my hands to my mouth, bowing my head like I was trying to stay out of it. I shouldn't have enjoyed listening to them bicker as much as I did, but I couldn't help it.

Ben never got mad; he just dug in his heels. When Collette finally realized she wouldn't get her way, she disappointed me by flopping onto the stairs in surrender. "Bring it to Iris's tomorrow, then." Her mouth twisted, bitter in defeat. "After dark but before curfew."

Eventually, I'd learn that keeping my mouth shut wasn't the best way to get what I wanted.

Bristling, I slapped my hands on my knees as I stood, then tried not to cry out. That sunburn wasn't as numb as I thought. "Fine, except we're meeting at Collette's."

Collette stared at me like I'd grown another head, and

her snappishness came back. She knew she could boss me and get away with it. "We are not! Mama and Daddy will be home. Are you crazy?"

"Then meet at the cemetery." Ben threaded his way between us as he climbed the stairs, and to my surprise, he pulled my hair when he went past.

I rubbed the sting on my scalp and looked back at him. I hadn't wanted to bring the board into it at all, but Ben had helped me get half my way, at least. Still, I couldn't tell if he was on my side or Collette's, so I didn't know if I should be grateful. His smile and shrug as he let himself into his house didn't clear it up, either.

&

When I got home, I clung to the rail like an old lady as I climbed the stairs to my room. My legs glowed like embers, and my face felt stretched tight enough to split. I still couldn't believe I'd fallen asleep in the cemetery instead of casting a spell.

I concentrated on that instead of on Ben's pulling my hair. If I thought about that, I'd have to wonder about his taking up for me and making jokes with me, and I didn't want to. Ben was Collette's concern, not mine, and I knew if he ever liked me too much, that would be the last of my best friend.

It took forever and a day to waddle upstairs, and when I was almost at the top, I stepped on something round. For a second, I had that roller-coaster feeling—my stomach fluttered like I'd gone weightless—and I sucked in a sharp breath, feeling it pinch between my ribs.

Something sturdy and solid bounced down the steps, and when I looked back, I saw a rock coming to rest on the landing. I frowned at it. It didn't belong on the stairs, or even in the house, but I was too sore to go pick it up. I figured it wasn't going anywhere.

When I opened my bedroom door, I let out a little cry.

My curtains waved around the open windows, stirred by the coldest breeze I'd ever felt. Scattered everywhere, papers twitched and skittered across the floor, thrown off my desk and torn from my walls. My shelves were bare, the books in fanned heaps on the floor, my prisms tossed like dice. In the middle of it all, more rocks than I could count covered my bed.

All that fire on my skin died; I crackled like February ice.

I missed the doorknob twice before I managed to grab it and slam the door shut. Something crashed inside my room. I didn't care. Whatever it was, it was locked in and away from me.

I ran down the hall. Every step was an earthquake up my spine. Aftershocks came when I threw myself into Daddy's room and slammed that door, too.

His dark damask curtains stirred, swaying toward me. They seemed alive, like they wanted to grab me and wrap me up. I scrambled across the bed to get away.

Grabbing the phone, I shut myself in Daddy's closet and slid all the way to the back, onto a pile of old boots. It was stuffy beneath the canopy of his work shirts; I couldn't breathe in the dark.

But I could dial, and I did.

&

I tried not to count how many neighbors had come out to watch when the police cars stopped at our house instead of at the Delancies'.

Deputy Wood sent me to wait on the porch while he searched the house with the state trooper who'd shown up right after him.

I heard them moving around inside and saw lights go on room by room. I heard them laughing, too. My cheeks burned twice, once with the sunburn and then with an embarrassed flush.

It seemed stupid now, calling 911 over a bed full of rocks, but I couldn't undo it.

Rennie Delancie shot me a smile when I caught him hanging off his front porch for a look. I wondered if he'd ever felt puny like this when the sheriff came to his door.

My heart sank when I saw headlights coming down our street. The last thing I needed was more police. They didn't send that many for Rennie, and he set off homemade bombs on a regular basis.

I was relieved and horrified when I heard a familiar crunchy squeak of brakes, then saw my daddy running up the walk.

Babbling, I ran into him the same time he ran into me, and I hid my face in his shirt. Everything came out in a rush, how somebody must have gotten into the house to destroy my room and how I'd hidden in his closet until the police came.

Daddy stepped back, his hands on my arms as he looked me over. "Are you hurt?"

"No, sir." I shook my head, gulping humid breaths that

got more ragged with each pull. It didn't occur to me until then that I hadn't called him.

"Stay put," he said, and went inside to talk to the police. Sinking down in our swing, I wrapped my arms around myself, scuffing the porch with my toes until I could hear the police coming down the stairs again.

"Seems like an awful lot of trouble to go through for a prank," the trooper said.

Deputy Wood laughed. "Well, what the hell else does Rennie have to do?"

Stung, I cooled my cheeks with my cold hands. I *knew* I should have just called Collette and had her help me clean up.

The police managed to plaster on sincere looks by the time they got to the door.

Deputy Wood bent down to talk to me face to face. "We checked everything out from top to bottom, darlin', and there's nobody in there now."

Minding my manners, I said, "Thank you."

"Do you know anybody who'd want to pull your leg?" Deputy Wood glanced at the trooper, who unfolded a piece of paper.

"No, sir," I said, straining to see what the trooper had.

Reassuring me, Deputy Wood said, "Nobody's gonna be in real big trouble, but breaking into houses is serious business. Even if it was just a joke."

Baffled, I shook my head again. Only Collette would care enough to prank me, and she couldn't be on Ben's back stoop and filling my bed with rocks at the same time. "I can't think of anybody, sir."

"You don't think Rennie Delancie might have come over here?"

I shook my head. "No. Why would he?"

"Why would anybody?" Deputy Wood asked.

The trooper smoothed the paper in his hand and held it out to me. "We found this; maybe you recognize that handwriting?"

Glancing over the note, I almost threw up in my lap. I recognized the tiny block letters, and I recognized the message, too.

Where y'at, Iris?

I didn't need my hands to cool my face anymore, but what could I say? "Yessir, I know who wrote that—Elijah Landry did. A dead boy I raised up on accident is stalking me. No, sir, I do *not* need a straightjacket, thank you."

Rasping apologetically, I said, "I don't know it. I'm sorry."

Deputy Wood shook his head slightly, then stood up. "You let me know if you hear something."

After the police left, Daddy sighed. "I reckon we have a mess to clean up."

"I guess so."

Still, I lagged so he could go ahead of me. If there were any more surprises up there, I wanted him to find them first.

&

The next day, I needed an RC and some peace. I scrounged a dollar from Daddy's change jar, mostly in nickels and dimes. I figured he'd miss the quarters. With that and the last of my allowance, I waded through sticky heat to the Red Stripe.

Up on the main drag, a couple of boys were playing soccer in the street with a time-smoothed basketball. The ball gave a defeated sigh, too hopeless to echo like the boys' voices did. They yelled and called each other names, starting with "pansy" and working their way up until they saw me.

They wore the same faces my neighbors had when they'd been watching the police on my doorstep the night before. No more throwing rocks; no, they were interested now.

They mumbled when I passed, their murmurs a haze of gnats around my head.

"S'up, Iris?"

"Where y'at?"

I kept my attention on the pavement in front of me. At the faded splash of red on the curb, I ducked into the Red Stripe and headed straight for the coolers in the back. I was pulling out a soda when a hand fell on my shoulder.

Startled, I yelped.

"Sorry," Ben said, "I thought you heard me."

"It's all right."

Ben leaned against the next cooler over. "Still kinda jumpy about last night?"

"What about it?" Sliding open the door, I studied all the bottles. I figured if I seemed busy, maybe he'd leave me alone.

Ben frowned. "With the police and all."

I dropped my change on the counter and tried to escape. Any other time, I could buy a soda in peace and take it home without talking to anybody once. The Ondine grapevine was working full-time, though, because Collette flew up on me as soon as I got outside.

She dug her nails into my arm and hauled me around the building. "What happened? I wanted to call last night, but Mama told me to let it be!"

"Dang, Collette, leave some skin," I said. I peeled her claws out of my arm, then groaned when I saw Ben come out the back.

He heaved a bundle of boxes into the trash, then wiped his hands on his apron. When he saw us, he brightened, leaning over quick to shove a block in the back door.

A perfume of spoiled milk and hot, ripe cantaloupe tainted the air. There were probably worse things in the world to smell than a grocery's Dumpster, but I couldn't think of any right then.

"Are you hiding from us?" Collette asked me.

"No," I said, and raised my bag. "I just wanted to drink this before it got hot."

Everything went quiet, except for the cicadas. Collette shot a dubious look in Ben's direction. "So drink it already. Nikki was all up in the diner this morning saying you got a death threat and the FBI was probably gonna come, and all I could do was go, 'Well you don't know everything, so keep your mouth shut.' "

I'd meant to keep the note Elijah had written a secret. My chest felt full of cold lead weights when I thought about it. Nikki lived way out in the trailer park—if she knew enough to get it *that* wrong, I figured I should clear it up for Collette, anyway. Then, if she got to punching anybody, at least it would be over the truth.

"I don't want y'all to yell at me," I said.

"Why would we yell?" Collette asked.

Ben shook his head. "We won't. I won't."

"I'm just saying, promise."

Exasperated, Collette swept her fingers across her chest. "There."

Wrapping both hands around my soda, I dragged my lip through my teeth and made myself say it. "It was Elijah."

Collette ticked her head forward. " 'Scuse me?"

"He was in my house. He filled my bed with rocks and tore everything all up." Hunching my shoulders up to my ears, I looked from Ben to Collette. "He left a note, too. All it said was, 'Where y'at Iris?' so I knew it was him."

"The police did not come to your house over a ghost!"

"See?" I told Ben.

"I'm not yelling," Collette insisted. "I'm just talking loud."

"You still got the note?" Ben sounded hopeful.

I shook my head. "The police took it."

"Course they did," Collette said.

Taking a slug of my soda, I wheezed when the bubbles hit the back of my throat just right to make my nose burn. "They did. We've been looking for Elijah all summer. How come you don't believe me?"

"Maybe 'cause it's just playing." She took my soda for a drink. "Nothing came up out of the lake when we called, did it?"

I could have stood stark naked in the street and felt less bare than I did right then. How funny was it, how awful, that Collette had stopped believing right when something real finally happened? She had to believe me, and I figured the only way to get that was to tell the whole truth, no matter how bad it made me look.

"I lied about the lake."

Ben stared at me. "How's that?"

"I pushed, on the witchboard."

"Aw, Iris," he said.

Ashamed, I slumped against the wall. Splaying my arms, I looked toward the sky. They probably weren't gonna give me any Hail Marys, but I had to confess.

"I saw him in the graveyard that first time; that's true. And he moved my spellbook and wrote in it when I wasn't even home. There was a dream and this. But the witchboard wasn't working, and y'all wanted it to, so I pushed. All up till the end; then he did the last part. I'm not lying about anything else. I swear to Mary and Jesus and God and everybody."

"What dream?" Collette asked. Like she couldn't help herself. Or maybe like she believed me.

Peeling the label off the bottle, I stared at it instead of up at them. "I followed a butterfly down to the river, and when I got there, he was skipping rocks, smiling at me."

Collette tugged my sleeve. "Did he say anything?"

" 'Where y'at?' " I murmured, suddenly full of cold.

"That's all?"

I closed my eyes and nodded. I didn't know how to make them understand that that one little question was enough.

&

When Ben got done at the store, he and Collette invaded my house.

"Most everything's out back," I said, shooing them off the porch. I had to untie the trash can lids to give them a look at my broken picture frames and shredded posters.

Picking up one of my fractured ballerinas, Collette frowned. "You love this one."

I nodded. Looking at all my things again in daylight, I wasn't so much scared as hurt. He'd smashed them all up for nothing, for spite.

A twitch went up my spine when I heard rocks whispering and chittering together. Turning, I watched Ben sift his fingers through the wheelbarrow's bin.

"That's them," I said. I put a hand on Ben's to stay him, to quiet those stones.

Collette picked one up, turning it over. It was nothing special, just a gray old river rock worn smooth by water. She tossed it back in the pile and said, "Go get your spellbook. I wanna see what he wrote."

"My daddy's sleeping," I said, hoping that would be the end of it.

"We know," Collette said. "We'll wait out here."

She didn't move; I didn't move. Not until Ben ran his fingers through the stones again. The slick hiss and click drove me right inside. I tiptoed up the stairs and clutched the book to my chest as I came back down, one foot on each step, as slow as I could.

Even though I was relieved to have all the truth out, I had a hint of heartsickness over it. For a while, just a while, Elijah had been all mine.

As soon as I stepped off the porch, they scrambled around me. Ben leaned over my shoulder, and Collette hung on my arm, waiting eagerly to see my proof.

Flipping to the page, I mumbled, "I thought I imagined it at first."

Ben shook his head in wonder, reading aloud. " 'How to Talk to Elijah.' How about that?"

Running her fingers over the page, Collette exhaled in amazement, then jerked her head up. "That's why you got sunburned!"

"No, I got sunburned 'cause I fell asleep."

Ben touched my shoulder, and he dipped his head to look at me. "You all right?"

It felt low to shrug him off, but I didn't want him touching me.

"I'm fine. I'm just tired. It took me and Daddy half the night to clean up his mess."

"Oooh, you think Elijah's jealous?" Collette lit up with that idea. "What if he's talking to you because he's in love with you?"

As far as I knew, and I didn't know a whole lot, love wasn't supposed to leave you crying in a closet with the police on their way. I shook my head. "No offense, Collette, but that's about the dumbest thing I ever heard."

"Why else would he come up into your room?" Collette persisted. "He didn't come up into mine or Ben's, did he, Ben?"

"Nope." Ben flipped backward in my spellbook to read the other pages. So much for our secrets; so much for our curse on the first page.

"And he didn't leave us love notes. . . ."

Making a face, I cut her off. "They're not love notes!"

"Close enough." Collette turned her gaze slowly, letting it linger on Ben for a minute before she went on. "And he calls you by name. It takes a lot of energy for a ghost to talk, and he always uses some when saying your name."

"It's only four letters," I said. "It's not like I'm Penelope or Elizabeth or anything."

"Or Evangeline," Ben added, waving the book slightly. "Do any of these work?"

Collette looked like she might yank it right out of his hands. "They all work if you do 'em right."

Turning the notebook around, Ben held it up to show our spell for invisibility. "No kidding? I could use this one."

Seeing a chance to change the subject, I threw in the part Collette left out. "It's only good if nobody looks at you, though."

Ben smiled, and suddenly I did, too.

"Anyway," Collette said, holding her hand out for the spellbook, "whatever it is, you've got a connection, so we should do the board at your house."

I gaped at her. "He's already riled up—you want to make it worse?"

Collette shrugged. "I think he's just frustrated."

Seeing as how Elijah came and went as he pleased and could cart a whole riverbed into my room if he felt like it, I didn't see how *he* was the one who was frustrated.

chapter seven

&

The inside of Nan Burkett's trailer smelled sweetly artificial, like apple spice from a can.

Rose-patterned curtains covered the windows, matching the dusk-pink couch and creamy carpet. Curio shelves held a collection of porcelain Scarlett O'Haras, with the occasional kitty thrown in for variety.

"I have red pop and lemonade," Miss Nan said, gesturing for us to sit down. When she walked, her hips swayed back and forth, her tight denim skirt whispering with each step.

I was pretty sure I caught Ben staring, but since I had been, too, I couldn't hold it against him. She was just plain interesting to look at.

We all took lemonade, which she brought to us in glasses with little ivy leaves ringing the rim. I thought I saw her add a little extra something to hers before she went back to a pile of laundry on her table.

"So," she said, picking up a white T-shirt with the ghost of a grease stain on it. "Y'all want to hear about Elijah."

Collette nodded in midsip, hurrying to swallow so she could answer proper. "Yes, ma'am. Everything you re-member."

Miss Nan smiled with her mouth closed, like she'd remembered a secret. "Well, first off, he was something to look at—long ol' eyelashes, the sweetest damned smile. His mama wouldn't let him wear his hair long, but he got enough in front to feather it."

She took a deep drink of her lemonade and picked up another shirt. "Anyhow, he was a boy. He ran all over, joyriding, playing stickball, sneaking into the movies. His mama didn't know about all that. There was plenty she didn't know."

Condensation trickled down my glass, giving me a good reason to have the shivers. Miss Nan's sunny face had clouded over, an old storm new all over again.

"Was she strict?" I asked.

"Oh hell yes," Miss Nan said, and reached for her glass. "Babette Landry had herself one perfect baby boy, and she planned on keeping him that way."

The hard edge in Miss Nan's voice made *Babette* sound like a curse.

Subtle as I could, I elbowed Collette. Ben had the sense to talk out loud. "How come?"

Fortifying herself with another swallow of lemonade, Miss Nan went back to folding. "She had him late, first, last,

79

and only. Elijah was a bandage baby, the kind a woman has to patch a marriage up when it starts falling apart."

We all nodded, and I leaned over my glass. "Did he hate her for it?"

I didn't mean to sound so hungry, but she knew *so* much. Gossipy things, real things—it was like eating sugar straight from the bowl.

Stopping midfold, Miss Nan trained a slow look in my direction. "Why do you care so much about old Elijah Landry? Your daddy been reminiscing?"

"Sort of," I lied bravely. My eyes watered when Collette pinched the side of my thigh. I'd have appreciated getting her approval without the bruises. "He just talked about the football team."

Hesitation weighted the moment. Miss Nan wrapped her arms around herself, clutching a blue dress shirt, for what seemed like forever. Then, like somebody'd flipped her switch, she started going again.

"Now, look. He loved his mama all right. All men do— you girls remember that—but the older he got, the less he wanted to be her doll baby. She had too many rules. No swimming because he might drown. No hunting because he might get shot. No driving because he might crash." Miss Nan tossed the shirt into the basket and reached for another, so bitter I could feel her prickle on my own skin.

"No girls because he might get one in trouble. She might as well have said no living, because that's what she meant. Babette wrapped him up in tissue paper, and she hated every one of us who tried to tear it off."

"If it's all right to ask, ma'am," Ben said, itching to hurry her, "were you there when he went missing?"

Grabbing a brown paper bag from beneath the table, Miss Nan shook it hard to open it. It rattled like caught thunder. "I was that boy's first and last kiss, Mr. Duvall."

Collette almost lunged off the couch she was so excited. "For real?"

"I was there the night before." The wistful look came back, and Miss Nan blindly stuffed shirts in the bag. "He'd been in the hospital. Babette didn't want us bothering him when he came home, but I snuck in anyway. Climbed right into his window and lay down beside him . . ."

"What was he in the hospital for?" I asked, on the edge of my seat. "My daddy didn't say."

Necklace glittering in the light, Miss Nan stopped, her pretty features smoothing. Escaped streaks of lipstick haloed her mouth. She waited a second, then said, "I don't know. Just sick, I guess."

We jumped when she punched the stapler three times fast to seal up the bag. Everything warm and cozy in Miss Nan's trailer bled away.

Feeling like intruders, we shifted uncomfortably, trying to talk to each other with our eyes, until Collette got brave. "All right, then, but what do you think happened to him?"

"I think his bitch of a mother killed him, that's what I think." She slammed the stapler once more, then thrust the bag at us. "Y'all run that over to Duane Jessee for me. Tell him it's a dollar more for the dress shirt."

&

After we dumped off Duane's laundry, we took our time heading to Ben's house.

"She was definitely drinking," Ben said, kicking an old split tennis ball into the weeds. "And she was lying when she said she didn't know why he was in the hospital."

Miss Nan had started out sweet and gotten mad so fast. . . . My head felt full, stretched tight with new information. "I know, she so was!"

Collette tugged a stick free from a tangle of brambles, using it as a cane. The wood bent under her weight, a curl of willow in her hand, but she seemed happy enough to keep going that way. "Still, I don't think Old Mrs. Landry killed him."

"Where'd you get that from? You can't just decide without evidence." Ben looked over at her, his frown suspicious.

"I have evidence." Whipping up dust with the end of her cane, Collette hurried ahead, turning so she could walk and talk to us at the same time. "In her heart, I imagine Miss Nan believes every word she said, but don't you think she told the police Elijah's mama did it? I would have."

"Maybe the police didn't care."

Ben and Collette turned on me like I'd gone soft in the head. They hadn't seen the look on Deputy Wood's face, though. They hadn't heard him laugh about it, like Elijah's going missing was nothing to worry about. "The police thought they were wasting their time looking for him. Why would they listen to her when they all thought he ran off?"

"They wouldn't," Collette gave her stick another twirl and fell into step with us. "We'll have to ask him."

"Where are we meeting?" Ben asked.

"My house." I would have rather met at the graveyard, but it was better to bend like Collette's willow cane than get snapped. I even managed to come up with a good side. "I can't get caught out after dark if I'm at home, can I?"

Ben shook his head, leaning forward to look at me past Collette. "I guess not. You don't plan on calling the police on me like you did Elijah, do ya?"

Snorting, I shrugged. I'd had enough embarrassment on my front porch to last me a good long time, but that didn't mean I couldn't have a little fun with it. "I might, so you'd best come to the door instead of sneaking in my window like you usually do."

Collette's quiet turned chilly, and I shrank. I didn't know why I'd said it. It just sounded funny to me: a big, foolish joke nobody could possibly take seriously. But she did. She had frost in her voice when she asked, "What time does your daddy leave for work?"

"Eight-thirty or thereabouts."

Tossing her cane into the bushes, Collette veered off when we got to the corner. "I'll be there at nine o'clock," she said. She hurried away with her head held high, leaving a little bit of winter in her wake.

chapter eight

&

I filled Daddy's thermos and tried to shove him out the door. My heart beat faster and faster. Though Daddy'd never said it was against the rules to have friends over while he was gone, I figured I'd be better off if I didn't give him the chance.

He kept dawdling and I didn't know why until he stopped at the door and asked, "Are you going to be all right alone?"

"Yes, Daddy, God!" I snatched his lunch off the counter and held it out at arm's length. "As soon as you leave, I'll lock up."

"I mean that. One call from Rennie Delancie in my lifetime is more than I need."

Disappointment stuck in my throat. I'd been so happy thinking Daddy'd just known to come home and save me; it hurt to find out he hadn't. I guess I should have known better. Daddy didn't believe in that sort of thing.

I shooed him toward the walk. "If you're late, it's not my fault."

Pointing as he jogged down the steps, he called back, "I mean it! Lock that door!"

And I did, for the whole ten minutes it took Collette and Ben to show up.

"He didn't bring the board," Collette said, brushing past me. It was still winter in her world; she didn't even bother with a hello.

Ben followed, arguing with the back of Collette's head. "It's not my fault! Shea told her I had it and she took it back!"

"You shoulda hidden it," she snapped. "You shoulda left it at my house."

"I didn't want to leave it at your house!"

"And see where that got us?"

Leaning against the door to close it, I wanted to slide to the floor and mope. Nonna's witchboard was the finest thing about Ben Duvall, and now it was gone. I twisted the lock until it caught, barely looking up at them. "So what are we gonna do?"

"Nothing, now," Collette said, black and dire.

"You got some candles?" Ben hunched down in his Saints jersey, hands stuck in his pockets. "We could have a séance if you got candles."

Collette snorted.

"What?" Ben glared at her. "You got a better idea?"

"You don't listen to my good ideas."

Before things got really ugly, I said, "We've got storm candles, lots of 'em." I started for the kitchen, tugging one of Collette's curls. "Help me carry some drinks?"

"I'm not thirsty," she said, then winced when I yanked her curl hard.

"We might be later." Narrowing my eyes, I stared at her until she got up to follow me.

In the kitchen, I pulled glasses out of the cabinets while Collette got the ice. Glancing to make sure Ben hadn't moved any, I lowered my voice to a whisper. "Collette, you know I was only joking."

"I know *you* were." She set the ice bucket down hard, scattering flecks and chips all over the counter. She'd been coming to my house long enough to know which drawer had the washrags in it, and she grabbed one to clean up her mess. "It's not just you."

Rooting through the drawers, I asked carefully, "What did he do?"

"I don't even know how to explain it," she said. After scooping the ice chips into the sink, she tried filling the glasses again, more slowly this time. "Half the time, he's all over me, and half the time, I don't even know why I'm there. I don't get him at all."

"He's probably wound up about his mama," I said.

Collette flattened her hands on the counter. "He could talk to me about that, but he don't. He'd talk to *you*, I bet."

"Uh-uh," I said automatically, but my stomach sank. He probably would have, if I'd let him.

I didn't know how to give Collette advice about stuff like this. Since she was mad, I figured I couldn't do wrong by appealing to her temperament. "He's gonna be sorry he messed with you."

"I know. I don't care." Collette sighed, then said, "He's got a lazy eye, anyway."

Not that I'd ever seen, but I kept that to myself. I dug out the thick yellow emergency candles, then shifted deep in the drawer to find the matches. "He smells like cabbage, too."

"I can do better." Tumbling ice into the last glass, she looked at me and added grudgingly, "So can you."

She meant it, but she still looked wounded. Patting her hand, reassuring her one more time, I said, "I'm not looking, so it don't matter."

And with Elijah looking for me, that was the truth.

&

When we straggled back to the living room, Ben had cleared the coffee table so we could sit around it. He kept his eyes down, and I was careful to put his soda on the coaster instead of in his hands.

"All right, now what?" Collette lit a row of short candles as I arranged and rearranged.

Still on my feet, I turned off the lights, then hovered by the doorway. Upstairs, the hall light still burned, so we had candles and a faded orange glow to keep us from falling all over each other in the dark. "The AC's awful loud; y'all want me to turn it down?"

"It's fine," Ben said.

"I'm cold," Collette said.

I pushed it to seventy-five and flopped down at the head of the table, with Collette on one side and Ben on the other. We were as far away from each other as we could get while still sitting together. The amber glow from the candles filled our triangle.

"We're supposed to hold hands," Ben said, offering his, palms up.

Glancing at Collette, I asked, "How come?"

Ben sighed. "The Web page said."

Caught between knowing everything and shunning Ben, Collette twitched, then grabbed Ben's hand. "Same reason everybody does the witchboard together—it's so you don't get possessed."

"There you go," Ben said, relieved, and I joined the circle.

Collette's palm was still cool and damp from pouring sodas; Ben's was hot and sweaty, and he took it back twice to rub on the knee of his pants before we got started.

Clearing his throat, Ben stared at the candles but talked to me. "Elijah's your ghost, so I guess you'd better call him up. Just ask him to come down or something."

Inside my belly, my nerves tangled to a knot. It seemed kinda stupid to call down a ghost testy enough to trash my bedroom—but like I had when we played the witchboard, I just went along. It was easier that way.

I breathed through my nose, exhaling slow as I let my eyes drift closed. Ice tinkled in our glasses like chimes, and the steady hum of the air conditioner became a regular, electric heartbeat. "We're trying to talk to you, Elijah. Are you there?"

A busy silence answered. I could hear ordinary house sounds from about everywhere, but no word from the other side.

Gooseflesh prickled my arms, winding me up tight in anticipation. His voice had been clear in the cemetery; I was afraid that I would—and that I wouldn't—hear him again, right there in my living room.

Collette squeezed my hand and whispered, "Ask again."

I licked my dry lips. "Elijah, if you're there, answer me."

Something thumped above us, a rolling kind of sound, like somebody falling out of bed. My throat went desert dry, because we all three looked up at the same time. I wasn't the only one who heard it.

Hushed, I tried again. "Elijah, 's'at you?"

The hair on my arms stood up when the ceiling rumbled again. I felt like I was breathing through water, and I know I squeezed Collette's hand too hard, because she gasped. I couldn't help it, though. Those sounds were coming from my bedroom.

"Elijah, do you have a message for us?" Collette asked quickly, as if somebody might stop her if she didn't rush it all out.

The living room filled with the sound of marbles skimming across hardwood. Rattles and jumps and bumps went on and on—an answer, but not real specific.

Eyes wide, Ben spoke to the ceiling. "If that's you, Elijah, knock once for yes and twice for no."

Startled, Collette squeaked at two sharp raps, right up close.

"Elijah Landry, is that you?" I asked.

One knock.

"That's yes," Collette said. Her voice came out thin, broken with an uneven breath. Collette—the brave one, the one who'd wanted to pierce the veil between the living and the dead in the first place—all the color had gone out of her face. Her lips had turned hazy gray, and that scared me. I wanted to cry.

"We ought to stop," I said.

Collette shook her head. "No. Keep going."

Agreeing with her, the ceiling thundered again, this time with heavy footsteps. Suddenly, I couldn't stop shivering; it had turned cold, so cold my bones ached. Any minute, I expected to see my breath frost up. "Do you have a message for us, Elijah?"

Two knocks. No.

Scared or not, Collette wasn't about to let foolishness ruin the moment. Sounding like our English teacher, she pronounced her question with perfect diction, demanding a real answer this time. "We're trying to help you, Elijah. Do you have a message for us?"

He rapped twice, then twice more, then just pounded away, slamming my bedroom door open and closed. Then everything stopped.

Looking around slowly, I chewed my bottom lip, wondering if we'd driven him off forever.

"Guess that's that," I said, and blew out the candle closest to me.

First, I heard the scream. It came so sharp and high, it broke my skin open and made me bleed ice cold. Dripping wet, my cheek burned. I touched it, and my fingers came back stained watery dark. I tasted salt and metal; the pressure in the room changed.

Collette picked something up from a pile of ice cubes and broken glass on the table. She turned it over, a smooth, gray stone dripping with pop, not blood. All at once, Collette croaked, then bolted for the bathroom.

I touched the spot on my burning cheek again, smearing the wet across my face as I tipped my head back to look at the ceiling. There wasn't anywhere for that rock to have come from, to crash down into Collette's glass like that.

Breathing fast, Ben slid closer to me. "Iris, you're bleeding."

"I know," I said. I put my hand on his shoulder and stood. Down the hall, I could hear Collette crying in the bathroom. "Go check on her; I'll be fine."

His hand strayed close to my face. "Iris, I—"

"Just go on, all right?" I brushed him away and turned, unsteady on my feet. I headed to the kitchen for a Band-Aid. I had no idea what waited for me upstairs, but downstairs I had glass, blood, and a broken best friend.

Elijah was a wild thing, and a mean one, and I'd had enough.

chapter nine

&

After Ben and I checked upstairs to make sure there were no surprises waiting for me, I made him promise to walk Collette all the way home. I managed to get them to leave through the back door. I had a funny feeling somebody was watching the house.

I locked the door, tugging the knob twice to make sure it stuck, and then headed into the living room to finish cleaning up Elijah's mess. I caught a glimpse of myself, pale and blood-smeared, in the window.

It was hard to keep my hands from the nick on my cheek once I saw it. It wasn't much bigger than a beauty mark, but it felt like a gouge, gaping down to the bone. I made myself shrug it off; I turned and started sweeping shattered glass into a grocery bag.

I'd only seen Collette that sick when cherries were in season. That, and my sunburn, and having the police to my house—it was all Elijah's fault. My temper grew the longer I scrubbed at the pop stains in the carpet.

Elijah'd turned Miss Nan into an old drunk and had driven his mama crazy, so as far as I was concerned, he could go back to purgatory, where he belonged.

It felt like freedom to tell him to go away. *Go away, you old bag of bones; nobody cares about you anymore.* I sang that under my breath as I picked tiny shards of glass from the carpet. *You're dead and gone.*

Inspecting the living room, I rearranged Daddy's magazines to hide the dull spot the spilled pop had left on the coffee table; then I went upstairs to take a shower. Lathering carefully around my sunburn, I felt older inside, like I'd been tested and passed.

Without Elijah, I had a whole summer to myself again. It would be all right if me and Collette read magazines all day long. We could fight over the quizzes in the back and go online to pick places to live when we finally got out of Ondine.

Wearing my new self proudly, I just stared when I stepped out of the shower to find a handprint in the steam on the mirror. Beads of water trickled from the ragged edges of the print; in the curve of the palm, I caught a hazy glimpse of myself gaping. All I could hear was that awful scaled rasp of stones pouring on stones.

I smeared my hand across the glass. "Go away," I said.

I got dressed and slipped into bed, tugging a blanket corner across me before closing my eyes. Nothing ever happened in Ondine, and I planned to prove it.

Nothing happened that night in my room, either, but no matter how hard I tried, I couldn't fall asleep.

Watching day grow brighter through my windows, I'd just gotten tired enough to drift off when the phone rang. I turned over and covered my head with a pillow to ignore it. The shrill didn't stop, though. I swore that it rang for five whole minutes before I finally answered.

Silence filled the line for a moment, then a voice asked, "Iris?"

I frowned. "Yeah?"

"This is Ben," he said, concern coming through. "Did I wake you up?"

A quick look at the clock told me it was barely eight. Decent people never called before noon unless somebody'd died or had a baby. Irritated, I rolled over. "No. What do you want?"

"Just, you know, to say I'm sorry I didn't stay to help clean up."

"It was one glass."

"I know, but still." His voice hedged, cut with a hesitation that made me nervous.

"All I needed was for you to walk Collette home. It's fine."

"My daddy's got a bunch of boxes from high school in the attic, if you want to come look through them," Ben said. "You and Collette, I mean."

It made me mad, the way he jumped up to be my friend when Collette didn't want anything to do with him. "Nope. I'm done with Elijah."

"What? Why?"

Sunlight suddenly streaked through the window, the

morning rise finally getting past the trees. I watched dust dance on the light and stirred my fingers through it to make it spin. "He's mean."

Ben snorted. "I'd be mean, too, if I couldn't rest."

"Then I'm not coming to look for you if you disappear, either."

"Who asked you to?"

"Good thing you didn't."

Being done with Elijah meant being done with Ben, too, and I'd have to pull him off like a Band-Aid, quick and sharp, no matter how funny I thought he was. "I've got chores to do."

"Sorry I called," Ben mumbled, then hung up.

I listened to the line buzz for a minute. The quiet filled my ears, and the cut on my cheek throbbed in time with the ache starting behind my eyes. Finally, I hung up, too.

&

That heavy, empty feeling refused to go away. I spent the morning doing my chores as slowly as possible, then wasted the rest of my time before lunch peeling my room down to its core. I planned to scrape all evidence of Elijah out of there; I would use the leftover paint in our shed to make everything new again.

Halfway through sanding my old white desk, I nearly had a heart attack when I heard a door close downstairs. A tight band closed around my throat. I never noticed how fast I could get dizzy before, but it was like I couldn't think.

My body moved, though. It started for Daddy's room,

and I was just about to bang on his door when I heard my uncle Lee's voice rumbling up the stairs.

"Where's my chickpea?"

Relieved and tumbling over myself to get to him, I crashed down the stairs and right up to my uncle Lee. He smelled like ginger, and his hug was exactly what I needed.

"You didn't say you were coming!"

Uncle Lee grinned as he nudged me toward the kitchen. "I move in mysterious ways. Where's my lazy brother? Still in bed?"

"Yes, sir."

I smiled when I saw the box on the kitchen table. Uncle Lee was the king of tag sales, thrift stores, and clearance outlets, and every so often, he'd roll in with a box of treats for me. Clothes and detective stories, Belgian cookies in gold tins, and one time, a silver gel pen and a pad of black paper. I always kind of hoped for another one of those pads, because I liked it too much to use up.

Leaning back on the counter, Uncle Lee watched me dig through the latest collection. "There's some catalogs and old pictures in the bottom, but those can wait. Catch me up—what's new?"

"Well, let's see," I said, then stopped at a soft red shirt in the middle of the box. It had a V-neck and swirling sleeves and a tie around the middle. Ducking into the downstairs bathroom, I talked through the door as I changed. "Collette's all bent out of shape about Ben Duvall."

Uncle Lee laughed. "Is that so?"

I tugged the new shirt over my head, shivering at the cool, silky fabric on my skin. "It's messed up. She wants us to hang out together. Then when we do, she gets mad if he's nice to me. And gets mad at me if I'm *not* nice to him. Now I think they're broke up, so who knows?"

"Let's see it," Uncle Lee said. I stepped out of the bathroom and he slipped his hands into his pockets, sighing. "Lord, don't you look grown?"

Smoothing the shirt with my hands, I looked down. "I guess so."

"Take my word." Uncle Lee pushed off the counter.

I turned and let him fix the tie. "So what do I do?"

"About Collette? Nothing."

Looking over my shoulder, I frowned. "That's not advice."

When Uncle Lee let go, he rubbed his hands. "In a couple years, Ben'll be a punch line to a joke only y'all two know. Until then, nothing. She can't hold nothing against you."

"You don't know Collette," I said.

Uncle Lee made a face as he pulled his keys from his pocket. "Where'd that mouth come from? C'mon, let's go for a joyride."

&

We didn't eat out much; Daddy said that for what most folks spent on fast food in a week, we could cook our own dinners for a month, so we did. That made going to a restaurant a special occasion.

Uncle Lee let me pick, and I chose the teahouse out on the river. From my window seat, I could see the water drifting by. The sunlight on the waves hypnotized me, dancing like fireflies, glimmering like stars.

With a low, disapproving sound, Uncle Lee tapped my foot with his to get my attention.

"Don't you fall in love with the river," he said. "First it's the river, then it's the rivermen. Then the next thing you know, you're on the run with a gambler, crying when he loses your wedding ring in a hand of five-card stud."

I picked up my menu, fanning it lazily in front of my face. "Oh really? Is Uncle Carl a gambler?"

"Hardly." Uncle Lee snorted, then sat back. "Look now, maybe I fell in love with an accountant, but take my word. I still know everything."

Feeling like I had nothing to lose, I said, "Then you know about ghosts."

"I do."

"So tell me." Real quick, I added, "About a real one; I don't care about make-believe anymore."

"You probably don't remember Granny Boone, but she was my favorite." He shushed me from ever sharing that secret before he went on. "When I was at school at Tulane, I woke up one night and saw her standing at the foot of my bed. I thought it was strange that she was there, but I wasn't scared. She smiled at me and told me to go back to sleep, so I did. About a half hour later, Jack called to tell me Granny'd passed."

A quick shiver ran through me, and I stopped fanning my menu. "Really?"

"Yes, missy." Uncle Lee nodded. "Our family's so full of ghosts, we could rent 'em out two for a dollar. Uncle Bobby got a call from his wife the day *after* her funeral." He put his menu down as our waiter approached. "Then again, Uncle Bobby thinks the CIA is stealing his trash. I don't know that you can take that one for the gospel."

I ordered, then willed the waiter away so I could get back to my haunted family. "Who else?"

Uncle Lee leaned back and said, "You tell me."

There was that tone that said he knew, that said I could confide in him. Breathlessly, I said, "I saw Elijah Landry in the cemetery."

Uncle Lee's smile changed; it turned shaded and thoughtful. "Is that so?"

I realized if Daddy knew him, Uncle Lee must have, too. "Y'all got on?"

Squeezing lemon into his sweet tea, Uncle Lee nodded. "He was Jack's best friend. What makes you think it was him?"

"He said so. He wrote me a note. And I saw pictures in the newspaper; I know it was him. He wants me to find him. That's what we've been doing this summer."

"How about you back up," Uncle Lee said.

So I did, to the beginning. All through étouffée and first coffee, I spilled it out, until I had nothing left in me but a lingering doubt. Turning my glass with the tips of my fingers, I asked, "Am I crazy?"

"No." Uncle Lee shook his head. "Papa Charles buying four dead mules on purpose, that was crazy. This is just wound up."

Uneasy, I pulled my chair closer to the table. "It's true, though."

"I believe you," he said. "But I'm glad you're done with it. What you're talking about, Eli wasn't like that. He had his moods, but he was kind."

The way he said it made me feel ashamed, like I'd been

99

caught talking about somebody behind their back. I fibbed and said, "Maybe it's not him, then. He could still be alive."

Uncle Lee set his napkin aside. "I think Jack would have heard from him." He slid the dessert menu in front of me. "Pick something with strawberries for me. I'll be right back."

"Wait, one more?" I touched his elbow, and he stopped beside me. "Why was he in the hospital before he went missing?"

Uncle Lee paused. "I don't remember, Iris. It was a long time ago."

Left alone, I swallowed up my thoughts and turned to look at the people around me. In a corner booth, a brown-skinned woman tried to coax mouthfuls of rice into a baby bent on making a mess instead.

The table closest to me had two older ladies who looked fresh from church. They wore bright red suits and hats to match, and if I leaned right, I could smell their perfume, sweet and powdery.

When the waiter returned, I ordered something chocolate for me and something strawberry for Uncle Lee. The waiter tapped his pen on his order pad as he walked away. After the waiter passed my table, a boy across the way waved at me, and my cheeks went hot. I glanced at my new shirt, wondering how grown I looked, then, curiously, raised my head again.

My lunch turned to stone in my belly. It was Elijah. He sprawled back in the booth, feet up, jeans covering his sneakers. He smiled, and I saw his mouth moving.

I didn't need to hear to understand him.

"Iris?"

I started, looking up to see Uncle Lee standing beside me, blocking my view. He had a friendly, curious lightness to his voice. "You woolgathering, darlin'?"

I shook my head, and the muscles felt so stiff in my neck I thought they might snap. That would have been something, to have my head roll right across the restaurant floor; the police would have a time trying to explain that.

Uncle Lee settled back, and I could see the table across the way again.

It was empty.

chapter ten

&

I might have been done with Elijah, but Collette had other ideas. She fell right into decorating with me like she'd waited her whole life to rearrange my furniture. My desk went to one side of the room and my bed to the other, but the shelves had to stay put. Even empty, they were too heavy for us to lift.

As we climbed on the mattress to tack my canopy up again, Collette tried to sound casual, though her eyes didn't meet mine. "I was thinking we could go to Ben's next. His daddy has tons of stuff from high school up in the attic."

"I know, he told me." Suspicious, I pressed my hands to the ceiling to hold my canopy in place. "I thought he had a lazy eye, Collette."

"It's just a *little* lazy." She shrugged, reaching down to grab another pushpin. She made herself impressively busy with a handful of them, rolling them in her palm before reaching up again. "Anyway, there might be clues up there."

I stared at her. "Like what? Class pictures? That's real helpful." I made a dismissive sound.

"You never know!"

"I'm pretty sure I do."

"Ben thinks there might be something."

Huffing a breath, I forgot to hold the canopy in place. It drifted down, shrouding me in navy blue that I brushed at impatiently. "What happened to you doing better, Collette? Is he back to kissing you or something?"

Collette got quiet, a guilty expression flickering across her fine features. Her dark eyes shifting back and forth, she finally shrugged in defeat, smiling a smile that begged me to be happy about it. By God, Ben Duvall had kissed her, and she wasn't complaining.

"I thought he smelled like cabbage."

"You did, not me."

Dropping to the bed, I let the canopy hang over my face like a widow's veil and I stewed. It wasn't fair for her to change her mind like that, not without telling me first. Worse, I already felt like I should apologize to Ben; I'd have to for sure if he and Collette made up.

"I don't want to look for Elijah anymore."

"Well, we have to, don't we?"

She sounded so matter-of-fact that I tugged the gauze back to stare at her. She just looked thoughtful, her mouth pursed slightly, like I'd caught her puzzling over algebra homework.

I shook my head. "Not if we don't want to, we don't."

"Iris, he's already set loose." Reaching up, Collette knotted her hair at her neck. "We stirred him up, and we have to put him back down again."

"*I* stirred him up," I corrected.

If she was right, I had a whole lifetime of rock showers and handprints on steamed glass to look forward to. One bad spell in the cemetery might have cursed me.

All decided, Collette fanned herself with a folder, leaning over to pick through Uncle Lee's box. "Ooh, anything good?"

"The shirt I'm wearing," I said. My room needed airing, so I got on my knees and climbed under my desk to plug in my fan again.

Leaning down, Collette waved a brown book at me. "Look what he put in."

"Hold on, Collette, dang." I bumped my head on the underside of the desk, but I forgot the hurt in an instant. One of Elijah's stones lay in the shadows; it felt cool and heavy when I slipped it into my pocket.

Then, quickly, I plugged in the fan and sat up. "All right, what?"

Collette turned the chair and sat above me, then handed over the book with a flourish. "Look at that."

Marveling at the neat handwriting on the inside, I took a shuddering breath. The fan's drone filled my ears, so my voice sounded far away, even to me. "This was my mama's."

"I know. How come Uncle Lee had it?"

It was a good question, but I was grateful that she didn't expect me to answer. It seemed like something I should have known, and I didn't.

Collette flipped past photos—my parents when they were young, posed on front steps and car trunks, their eyes squinting in the sun. We stopped at a grainy shot of them in front of a Ferris wheel. Daddy and Mama took up the middle, though Mama wasn't looking at the camera. She had her head tilted back and was smiling at Daddy, her arms around his waist.

Elijah hadn't been facing the camera, either. Though he had his arms wrapped around a younger, softer-looking Miss Nan, he gazed toward something in the distance.

I murmured in surprise when I realized he was wearing the same jersey he'd worn in my dream. That little sliver of truth felt like ice on the back of my neck.

"What else is there?"

Sliding to the floor to sit shoulder to shoulder with me, Collette spread the book so that half lay on my leg, the other half on hers, and she turned the pages with vicious efficiency. If the pictures didn't have Elijah in them, she didn't stop.

There were notes under some of the pictures. One was *Valentine Lake, Summer 1987*—Elijah and Daddy trying to start a campfire. Another showed Mama crossing her eyes while Elijah put bunny ears up behind her head—that read simply *Summer 1988*.

I wanted to trace my fingers over her words, in ink like blood, some living part of my mama suddenly unearthed. And there she was with the boy who was haunting me. Making faces with him. Laughing with him and Daddy.

The last picture in the book had all three of them in it— Daddy and Mama and Elijah, dressed up in church clothes and hats. Underneath it, Mama had written *Easter 1989*.

Leaning my head against Collette's shoulder, I turned the last page back and forth, gazing at them in their Easter best.

That was the last of them, the end of their saved memories. There were a few blank pages still in the book; Mama must have quit filling it when Elijah disappeared.

An unexpected touch of grief settled on me, and for a minute, I was afraid I might cry, afraid I wouldn't be able to explain why, either. I sat up too fast and got a deep breath of paint fumes.

Feeling dizzy, I slid to my feet and held my hand back to haul Collette up. "I'm gonna die in here. Let's go."

&

In the shade and quiet by the creek, we ran into Ben. Me on one bank, Collette on the other, we went around the old downed oak and there he was. His bare toes touched the edge of the water; streaked sunlight danced on his golden hair. He had his fishing pole propped between his knees, his dirty fingers working at a tangled lure. Lost in his own thoughts, he didn't look up.

Collette lit up when she saw him. She ducked around the tree, coming up with a smile on the other side. "What do you think you're catching down here?"

"Nothing but flies," he said. His smile dimmed when he looked past her and saw me.

My last words to him rattled in my head, echoing until they got so loud I wanted to shake them right out. I felt stuck, because I really needed to say something, but I didn't want to do it in front of Collette and give her the wrong impression.

Fortunately, Collette had plenty to talk about. I nodded along while she explained the memory book and how we had to court Elijah back, only carefully this time. In my opinion, she was hinting about the witchboard again, but Ben didn't volunteer it.

"Anyway," Collette said, breezing right past Ben's missed chance to be a hero, "we ought to look at the stuff in your attic, Ben. Maybe he'll show himself if we find something good."

I had to talk then. "We don't need anything. We just need me." I peeked up and nearly hit Ben's gaze.

"How do you figure?" Squinting one eye at me, Collette waited for me to squirm, but I didn't.

"He's following me." I stood on certain ground, my heart almost still with the truth of it. "He showed himself when I was out with Uncle Lee. And after y'all left my house last time, he put a handprint on my mirror while I took a shower."

From the corner of my eye, I could see Ben's expression turn amazed. He leaned in, shadows from the tree boughs rubbing his skin in restless patterns. "He did?"

I crossed my chest with my fingers, and Collette let out a held breath. At first, I couldn't tell if she was glad or annoyed.

"And this is all real?" she asked. "You swear?"

I nodded.

"Then I guess we have three questions we have to answer," she said, counting them off on her fingers. "Why was he in the hospital? How did he get out of his room? And where is he now?"

Smiling curiously at her organization, I reached out and pulled up her fourth finger, because she'd left out the most important question. "And what happened to him?"

Scraping sand from my shoes, I started up the path. "Why don't we start in Ben's attic?"

&

"Hey, look, he signed my daddy's yearbook," Ben said, twisting the red volume in his hands to show it to us, then turning it back to read aloud. " 'Stay cool, Eli.' "

Collette swiped a curl from her eyes, marveling at this message from the past. "He called himself Eli."

"That's what Uncle Lee called him, too," I said with a shrug.

Searching there felt like a waste of time once I found out that Ben's daddy barely knew Elijah and, worse yet, hadn't saved anything personal.

We'd found a couple of pictures and an old letterman jacket that smelled like mothballs, but most of the treasure consisted of old trophies and report cards. Collette had fun teasing Ben about his daddy's D in economics, but that was about it.

I was ready to call it off, and not just because we hadn't found anything. The only way that attic could have been hotter was if it caught fire. In secret, I wished I would faint, first, because I'd never done it before and wondered what it would be like, and second, because I thought passing out would be a real good way to end the attic search.

It didn't happen, though. I got hotter and sweatier, but my brain stayed awake, like it was determined to thwart me. I dumped a pile of English papers back in the box and stood up. "There's nothing up here."

"We still have four more boxes," Collette said with a whine. She gestured at a collection of milk crates that anybody could see had nothing in them but a bunch more papers.

Since I couldn't convince myself to faint, I said the first thing I thought. "Well, then you stay here. I'm going to Old Mrs. Landry's."

I sounded so sure that Ben and Collette both scrambled to their feet and followed me like rats after a piper. Of course, I got halfway down the street and wanted to change my mind. It would be a horrible thing to mess with an old lady, especially one who wasn't right in the head. My heart beat fast, then slowly, mixing up dread with shame, but I forced myself to walk. I'd made my first big move toward being the boss, or at least not being bossed anymore, and backing down would have ruined that.

My stomach got tight when we turned the corner. Old Mrs. Landry's house stood off from the others, its white paint peeling down to gray, the front screen pocked with holes.

The yard might have been tidy once. There was evidence of that, because flowers still grew along the paths, but they'd gone wild. Orange freckled tiger lilies nodded their heavy heads, and their green sword leaves scratched at the front steps, spilling into grass that needed mowing.

I rubbed my dirty hands on my jeans as I approached the front step. On a nail next to the door, a crucifix swayed, the pained, bleeding Jesus looking at me with sadness even though his eyes were closed.

Guilt rose up to choke me, and for a brief, hysterical

minute, I thought I might faint after all. I could hear the tiger lilies sanding the porch, Ben and Collette breathing behind me, and my own heartbeat.

Somehow I made myself knock, but I was so wound up listening to the tiniest things that I nearly screamed when Old Mrs. Landry appeared in the door.

Her face was pale, round as the moon, and she looked out at us as if she didn't understand something. Instead of opening the door, she grabbed the handle and held it closed. She blinked slowly, then asked in a dry, powdery voice, "What do you want?"

Somebody, most likely Collette, jabbed me in the back. I'd turned into some kind of puppet, because that nudge woke my tongue, and I heard myself talking from far away. "We wanted to ask you about Elijah, ma'am, if you wouldn't mind."

Old Mrs. Landry narrowed her eyes. "Who sent you over here?"

That wasn't what I expected her to say, so I looked back at Ben and Collette for guidance. Ben just shrugged, and Collette made a face like she was sorry. Before I turned back, I saw Collette reach for Ben's hand. He didn't push it away, and my heart sank. They were useless.

Facing Old Mrs. Landry again, I tried to meet her gaze, but the screen played tricks on my eyes. She looked close, then far away; then all I could see was a net of tiny gray squares.

Shaking my head to get my focus to behave, I shoved my hands in my pockets and said, "Nobody, ma'am. We're just interested."

"Oh, are you, now?"

I didn't recognize this Old Mrs. Landry; she was hard—not like the woman who traded candies for prayers on the church steps. Her teeth flashed when she talked, and her head twitched with each word, like it took her whole body just to say something.

Flattening herself against the screen, she raised her voice to a shout. "I guess you want a tour of his room, too? And if I wouldn't mind, could you have a drink out of his favorite cup? And if I'd be so kind as to give you something that belonged to him? That kind of interested?"

"No, ma'am, no. I just—"

"I know what you just!" Old Mrs. Landry swung the door open. Its rusted hinges screamed, and the frame hit my shoulder, knocking me down.

Struggling to my feet, I cringed when Old Mrs. Landry came down on me. Her fingers dug hard into my chin; she forced me to meet her eyes. Even in the heat of summer, her touch was cold.

"Jackie didn't take enough of my boy? Now he's sending his brat after a piece, too?"

I felt hands on my shoulders—Ben and Collette trying to drag me back. Ben kept whispering, "Come on," urgent and strained. My feet were stuck in place, though, and I think I would have stood there all day and all night if Old Mrs. Landry hadn't shoved me.

She didn't push hard, but it was enough to knock me off balance. I fell past Ben and slid against the walk, scraping my hands on the concrete. Collette hauled me to my feet again.

With her eyes open so wide that white showed all the way around the brown irises, Old Mrs. Landry raised a hand high over her head and screamed, "You get the hell away from my house!"

Collette yanked my wrist, dragging me down the walk. She didn't even look both ways as she shoved me across the street; she was too busy looking back to make sure Old Mrs. Landry wasn't following us. If walking up to the house had been in slow motion, running away from it was in fast-forward.

Everything blurred; I knew we'd started running, but we moved so fast I couldn't think or talk. I didn't feel sick until we collapsed at Collette's.

Angry, embarrassed tears stung my eyes, and I trembled when Ben and Collette crowded around me. Ben turned my hands over in his own, his touch soft as butterflies. That distracted me; it seemed wrong. His hands should have been rough and bandaged like my daddy's.

He slipped away from me, and I heard him say something about asking Mrs. Lanoux for some peroxide before the door wheezed shut. Rubbing my back, Collette leaned her head against mine and whispered comfort to me. She smelled like honey. "She's crazy, Iris. She's crazy."

I nodded but didn't say anything. I could still see Old Mrs. Landry's eyes, her hand rising to hit me, and that stole all the sound from my throat.

She wasn't just a little funny in the head. She *was* crazy, and still, I almost wanted to go back—*almost*—just to ask what pieces my daddy still had.

&

Collette sat beside me on the front porch. A brown bottle of peroxide was tucked between her knees. Pulling paper towels from her pocket, she snapped her fingers lightly at me, and I held out my hands.

"Told Mrs. Lanoux you got a splinter," Ben said.

Rooster ran circles around us. "That don't look like a splinter to me." He stuck his head down to peer at my hands, then bounced away when Collette shoved him. "I'm gonna have to tell Mama you lied."

"He didn't either," Collette said, indignant. "There's some splinters in there." Threatening Rooster with a half-raised hand, she glowered until he pinballed as far from me as he could go without leaving.

He picked a board in the porch and pretended to balance on it, putting one foot in front of the other with careful concentration. "I'm probably gonna have to tell."

Frowning, Ben caught him by the belt to hold him still. "How about you go inside and get us a soda? I'll give you a dollar."

"Dollar fifty," Rooster countered, swinging his arms in circles so wide he nearly hit Collette in the nose. "Plus tax."

Ben dug into his pocket and shoved crumpled green into Rooster's hand. "That's two. Now go on."

"You better not do that again," Collette said, though it didn't sound like she disapproved. "I can't afford to pay him every time I want him to go away."

I picked flecks of dirt out of my hand, then gritted my teeth as Collette poured peroxide over the scrapes again. White froth bubbled up instantly and stung. "Maybe we could save up and send him away for good."

Collette nodded. "I like that plan."

"I bet he'd walk to Sorrento for ten dollars." Ben grinned, then reached in to pat my hand with a paper towel.

Suddenly, Rooster came running back, tripping over his own feet. "The police are at your house, Iris!"

"That's not funny," Collette snapped.

"I'm serious!" Rooster jabbed a finger in the direction of my house. "There's two cars out front, with the lights on and everything!"

"Are you sure it's mine and not the Delancies'?"

When Rooster nodded, my insides ground to a halt. I stood and got my feet moving, though I wasn't sure how. Almost everywhere, I was numb, and where I wasn't numb, I was afraid. A single, awful thought repeated over and over again:

What have you done now, Elijah?

chapter eleven

&

Almost in tears, I burst into the house and nearly fell to my knees when I saw Daddy whole and healthy standing in the living room. Deputy Wood was there, with the same trooper who'd come when I called about the rocks. When they saw me, their smiles dimmed.

"What's going on?" I asked.

"Where have you been?" Daddy asked, his mouth a flat white line as he waited for an answer.

I could tell he wanted to fly up on me, his temper kept in check only because the police were there. Swallowing, I shrank. My voice cracked and I said, "Collette's."

Daddy's eyes turned darker. "Don't you lie to me, Iris."

"I'm not!" I exploded with a little more righteous indignation than I was due, but I hadn't lied. I *had* just come from Collette's. Pointing at the door I said, "Ask her!"

"Babette Landry says you were trespassing in her yard."

Deputy Wood raised a brow, waiting for me to deny it. Then he added, "And throwing rocks at her windows."

"I did not! All I did was knock on her door! I didn't throw anything!"

Daddy got harder by the second. "You're not helping yourself."

"I didn't throw any rocks!" Crossing my arms, I glared at all three of them and churned with hatred for Old Mrs. Landry. I wanted to throw up every cinnamon she'd ever given me. "Me and Ben and Collette walked up on her porch to ask her about Elijah! She's the one who went crazy!"

Instead of getting me out of trouble, that got me into more. Daddy looked at me in disbelief. "Now, why would you go and do something like that? What on earth is wrong with you?"

I thrust my hands up for him to see the scrapes, waiting for him to realize I was the victim, not Old Mrs. Landry. "I just wanted to ask what he was like, and she pushed me off her porch!"

Daddy turned cold. "Go to your room."

"But I didn't do anything!"

"I said go to your room!" Daddy roared so loud I could have sworn the pictures rattled on the walls.

I ran for the stairs, red-faced and furious, and stomped up them as loud as I could. Daddy could be mad all he wanted; I was madder, and I wasn't about to apologize.

&

From my window, I watched the police leave. I made faces at the back of Deputy Wood's head. If he was the best the sheriff's department had had to offer back then, no wonder they hadn't found Elijah.

Our neighbors trickled inside again, casting glances at our house just in case something else interesting happened. I climbed back onto my bed and stewed; they were all too nosy for their own good.

Rolling over to stare at my canopy, I decided I would tell Daddy exactly what Old Mrs. Landry said to me and about him. I heard him coming up the stairs and steeled myself.

"You all done pouting?" Daddy asked as he let himself in. He looked tired, with dark circles under his eyes and upset etched into the lines around his mouth.

I wrapped my arms around my knees faced the window so I wouldn't have to see him. "I wasn't."

After a quiet moment, Daddy sighed. "I want to know what's going on."

From his tone of voice, I knew I was getting grounded no matter what I said.

"I told you, we went up there to ask about Elijah, and she went crazy. Talking out of her head about touching his stuff and seeing his room and drinking from his cup." Hot and mad, I raised my hand and added, "She was gonna hit me."

Daddy turned my too-small desk chair around to sit in it backward. He kept shifting to catch my eye, but I wouldn't look up. "Why would you go over there in the first place? You know she's not right."

"I wanted to know why Elijah went to the hospital. I wanted to know what really happened."

Pain rose in Daddy's eyes, sudden and startled like I'd slapped him. In a blink, that sting turned steel, a flash of anger making his temple pulse. "Let me tell you something I think you need to get straight right here and now, sugar. Some things you ought to just leave alone."

"She thought you sent me." I held out my scraped hands, begging him to see. *Look—look what she did to me.* "What did you take, Daddy? She thinks you took something from him and sent me back for more."

Daddy paused. "She's a lost old woman, Iris, and you're fooling around with her memories. You're lucky shoving you is all she did."

That left me raw with disbelief. "You're taking her side?"

Daddy stood slowly, picking up my chair with one hand to slide it beneath my desk again. "I'm sorry you got hurt, Iris, but the woman's sick. You stay away from her from now on, you understand?"

"Maybe I would if you'd answer a question straight for once!"

"And what question is that?"

I dared to face him head-on and asked, "What do you have of Elijah Landry's?"

"Quit asking about him." Daddy walked out, leaving only his anger behind. "He's not a mystery for you to solve."

&

Daddy and I didn't talk at supper. We kept our war silence, and afterward, when I finished the dishes, I slipped upstairs. I had an inkling of a plan, so I figured I'd stay up there until he went to work.

I dumped all my Elijah things on the bed. I had my spells

118

and Uncle Lee's box and the lists of witnesses from the library. Reaching into my pocket, I added that single left-over river rock to the pile. Then, solemn, 'cause it was a ritual, I put in the picture of Elijah and my parents at the parish fair.

Looking over my collection, I had an itch in the back of my head, a blankish spot that stood for something, though I couldn't tell exactly what. I felt like I had missed an important clue. I was sure if I just stared long enough, it would turn bright and catch my attention.

The phone rang once, breaking my concentration, and then a minute later, my door clicked. I hurried to throw a cover over the pile.

Daddy didn't walk in, he just stood at the threshold and gestured with his thumb. "That's Collette."

"What, I'm not grounded?"

With the hint of a warning, Daddy asked, "Do you *want* to be?"

I dug my phone from under the bed, waiting until Daddy left before leaning against the door. He wouldn't sneak up on me again.

"Hello?"

"Oh my God, what happened?" Collette sounded breathless and flighty.

Rolling my eyes, I slid down the door, watching as pollen fluff drifted past. "Nothing, except Old Mrs. Landry is a big fat liar."

"Oh no," she moaned. "She called the police on us?"

"Well, she did on me, anyway. Told 'em I was throwing rocks at her house."

"Dang, Iris. Did you get in trouble?"

"I got yelled at." Raising my foot, I stirred the air to confuse the pollen fluff, making it spin wildly before I stomped it to the floor. "My daddy's leaving shortly; as soon as he's gone, you need to come over."

"Um . . . okay?" It came out like a question, thick with confusion.

Leaning forward, I opened my door enough to make sure Daddy wasn't listening on the other side before whispering, "Bring your books and just you; we're gonna find Elijah."

"You sure that's a good idea?" Collette asked.

"You're the one who said we had to put him down."

"But I didn't mean—"

"We need to quit messing around and do something, Collette. Come or don't; whatever."

She hesitated again, then said, "All right, I'm on my way."

℘

I stood candles up in teacups all around my room, lit them from a box of matches, then moved on to arranging my bed. The Ferris wheel picture lay on my pillow, and beside it, my spellbook. The library notes went back in my desk, but I put the rock in my pocket. I would need that.

"Lord, Iris," Collette said, slinking into my room. Candlelight shone under her dark eyes, shading them from below. She looked haunted as she turned in a slow circle.

With a measure of pride puffing me up, I waved my hand at the room transformed. "Looks good, don't it?"

Collette nodded.

"We're using the spell to talk to Elijah. I need you to hold my hand and pull me back in case something bad happens."

"Do you want me to chant anything?"

"If you want to. Something quiet and steady."

I arranged myself in the middle of the bed, nudging the picture back into place when it threatened to slide off the pillow.

Reaching into my pocket, I produced the rock. Elijah'd sent that to me; I figured it would help me find him.

I closed my eyes. This time, I wasn't afraid; I wasn't even anxious. I knew down in my soul Collette wouldn't let anything happen to me. Steadying myself, I squeezed the rock as I tried to sink to that shallow-breath place again.

I noticed the tiniest things. Wind kissed my curtains. Collette smelled like baby powder. The candlelight became solid in a way, a warm blanket coursing over my skin.

The drifting was just like the first time, when I lay on Cecily Claiborne's grave; just like the butterfly dream; but this time I was ready. I knew where I wanted to go.

Show me Elijah, I murmured inwardly. *Show me the last of him.*

My house washed away in watercolors, draining down to black, with me marooned in it. Then the walls came up again. An unfamiliar bedroom surrounded me.

Elijah sat at his desk, scribbling away on a piece of paper. He didn't notice me; he didn't even stop writing. Wads of tissues filled his trash can, and he blindly reached for a new one. Pressing it to his nose, it bloomed with a bright red spot of blood.

He was going to die soon. I felt it; it built like a storm cloud getting darker and darker until rain had to fall. These were Elijah's last minutes, and he couldn't hear me warning him to get away.

The window rattled and me and Elijah both turned to look at the same time. When I saw the face there, I choked. A sharp, sudden hook in my belly yanked so hard I thought I might tear.

In the time it took me to blink, Elijah disappeared—his room, his time, too—and the moon became Collette's face, staring down into mine.

"Iris?" Collette shook me.

I struggled to sit up; my head swam. For a minute, I felt like somebody'd stuffed my head with clay; I couldn't even think. Sick and dizzy, I wiped my nose and found it bleeding.

I tasted copper, and it hit me in a wave who I'd seen in that window, who was there the night Elijah Landry died.

℘

Poor Ben looked like he might jump out of his skin when he saw two girls climbing through his window in the middle of the night.

He threw down his Xbox controller and grabbed his robe. While Collette giggled, I rolled my eyes to the ceiling and tried not to look. It was kind of hard, though, because I'd never seen a boy in his boxers.

"Iris had a vision," Collette said, trailing her fingers along the edge of Ben's desk. I let her tell him the story; I'd been there—that was enough for me.

His wallpaper had little baseballs and footballs on it, and the border was Astroturf green to match his bedspread and curtains. He didn't have very many books; instead, he had uneven stacks of comics, mostly the horror kind, with titles dripping blood.

Collette looked all pink and out of place in Ben's room, but I liked it. If it had been any other night, I would have been happy to sit down with a comic or two, or a bottle of glue and a snap-apart model—maybe of the planets. I didn't care about cars or spaceships.

When Collette finished, Ben edged toward me, staring at my nose. "Are you all right?"

Just in case it had started bleeding again, I rubbed my knuckle against it. "Yeah, it didn't hurt or anything."

"You caught his nosebleeds, huh? That's kinda weird." Ben rubbed his palms together thoughtfully. "If that happened all the time, sure does explain why nobody cared about the blood on his pillow."

"I think it explains something else, though." This part I'd saved to tell myself. Leaning back to sit on the windowsill, I stuck my hand in my pocket to rub the smooth river rock. I wanted to be dramatic, to draw out what I'd realized until Ben and Collette both turned ashen and gasped, but I didn't know how.

"Y'all wanna know who was in the window?" Ben nodded, and when Collette looked up, I broke the news. "My daddy."

"Iris, that's crazy," Collette said, and with a bounce, she dropped to sit on the edge of Ben's bed. She threw me a look of barely disguised disdain. "Your daddy wouldn't kill anybody!"

That hook in my belly pulled again. "I was there the night Elijah died, and so was he."

Ben asked, "Are you sure, though?"

I didn't want to be—the thought of it barely fit in my head. But I'd been there. I knew. "How could I mistake him, Ben?"

"You could go to hell for saying that," Collette said.

"Not for telling the truth." I waved the rock at her, then stuck it back in my pocket.

Collette stood up. "It doesn't even make sense."

My voice sounded strained, like I'd swallowed hot tea too fast. "You saw those pictures of Elijah goofing with my mama. How he was always looking at her, how Miss Nan all of a sudden goes away."

"And? Even if he *was* crazy in love with her, so what, Iris?" Collette tried to dismiss me with a casual roll of her shoulders. "That doesn't make your daddy a homicidal maniac."

"No, but I know for sure that Elijah's mean, don't I?"

Ben hissed softly. "What if he got tired of watching them?"

"If he tried something . . . ," I said, and stopped. I couldn't find the breath to say it.

"Your daddy'd have to do something about it," Ben said quietly.

I had to turn away, drying my face on my sleeve before they saw me crying. I knew what I'd seen, and I wished I could burn it all to ash. Daddy was all I had.

Collette's flat voice pulled me from my thoughts. "How come you're just now figuring this out, now that we're at *Ben's?*"

I pulled open the window. "I knew before. I just hoped I was wrong."

Before I could get outside, Collette stopped me with a scowl. "Liar. You're making up stories, just like you did with the witchboard!"

It was a low blow, bringing up sins I'd already confessed, and her protest felt like a slap. "Excuse me?"

"No excuse for it." Collette ignored Ben's frantic waving to lower her voice as she walked up to me. She dug deep and pulled out something she knew would hurt. "You're just trying to be special, and you're not."

Once, I'd gone so high on the swings that I slid out and lost my breath when I hit the ground, and that was exactly what Collette's words did to me then. Gathering myself, I concentrated on the faded sports wallpaper, then managed to find enough breath to say, "Good night, Ben."

He might have said something back, but I didn't catch it. I'd already stepped out onto the roof, and I didn't look back.

I knew the truth. I hadn't picked Elijah; he'd picked me. It wasn't even my spell that set him loose, but Collette's. If I was special, it was because it was meant to be, and Collette would have to get over herself. She couldn't be first all the time.

The night around Ben's house smelled like honeysuckle, sweet and soothing, as I climbed down the trellis. I was careful not to let it bang when I jumped to the ground; if Ben got in trouble for having girls in his room, it wouldn't be because I got him caught.

I just hoped Collette had the sense to feel the same.

chapter twelve

&

When I called Collette the next day, she told me right over the phone that we weren't on speaking terms. I tried not to let that bother me. I wasn't about to apologize for the truth.

All along, I'd needed to go to Elijah—I hadn't realized that until my vision. I had to get close enough to let him show me where he rested; then I could kiss him goodbye.

And yet, thinking about what must have happened to put him in my daddy's path—it was strange to care about him still. To feel him everywhere I went.

He was strongest by the river. I sat on the shore and chucked rocks into it, making myself more like him. I blinked and held up a hand when a shadow fell on me. My heart jumped as I looked up into a boy-shaped silhouette, haloed by the sun. I settled again when he moved out of the glare and proved to be Ben.

He poked the ground next to me with a stick. "Can I sit down?"

"I don't own the river." I leaned back on my elbows to look into the water again.

Without a hint of grace, Ben flopped down at my side, crossing his arms over his knees and squinting into the distance. Sneaky patches of sunlight bared the pale freckles on his face.

"Smells like a storm's coming," I said to fill the quiet.

"Looks like it, too." He pointed out the hazy sky with his stick, then swirled it around in wide curlicues. I think he signed his name in the air before looking at me again. "Collette's still spitting mad this morning."

I rolled my eyes. "Like that's news."

Disappointed, Ben said, "I'm serious, though."

"Me too." Rolling onto one elbow, I acted like I was queen of the world. Since he looked so whupped, I decided to needle him about it. "So how much trouble are you gonna be in when she finds out you came to talk to me?"

Ben made a face, tossing his stick away so he could thread his fingers in his hair. "She's not my boss."

I laughed under my breath. He sounded like he was in kindergarten and looked close enough to pouting that I expected him to stick out his lower lip. "You better not tell her that."

"I don't even think she likes me," he said.

The sour in my belly soured my words. "Don't be stupid, Ben."

He turned his pale blue eyes on me, and from his brows to his chin, an unsettled wash of hurt crept across his face. "When did you get to be so mean?"

I licked my hand to scrub at my knees and offered up my only excuse. "I'm sorry. I've got a lot on my mind."

"You're not the only one." Everything about him seemed to darken, not with anger but with heavy thoughts that sloped his shoulders and bent his back. "This was a lot more fun when it wasn't real."

A touch of guilt twisted low in me, and I worked harder at wiping my knees. "I didn't mean to see what I did."

Ben nodded, then knotted both hands in his hair. Wheat-gold stalks of it jutted between his fingers, and I finally realized what Collette meant when she said he was pretty. He had long, dark lashes and a softness to his mouth that made me want to stare at it when he talked.

He stole a look at me, so sad, and then turned to the water again. "I wish you hadn't. It was good, getting to go away. Making things up."

I stopped in midswipe. "We didn't go anywhere."

Ben tightened his fingers in his hair, dragged down a little more by that invisible weight. "My daddy hits my mama. He did. Not anymore."

It was like falling, hearing a confession like that. I could only guess at what would make a man stop hitting, once he'd started. " 'Cause she's sick?"

Ben looked at me, hard. " 'Cause the last time, me and Shea held him down and told him what he'd get if he ever did it again."

"Oh no."

"We meant it, too."

A single thread of cold worked through my chest. I didn't know Ben's parents, but I'd seen them at church. They looked like happy people to me, Ben's daddy tall and gold, his mama true Acadienne, pale skin, dark hair. They held hands in the pews all the time. I didn't understand how those outsides could hide this inside.

I grasped for something, anything, to say. I tugged his wrist, making him free a hand so I could slip mine into it. I didn't even think about it; he hurt and I wanted to make it better. "I think you did a good thing."

"I can't even tell anymore." Ben looked at our joined hands; all I could see of him was the troubled curve of his brow. I thought he might be crying, but when he raised his head again, his face was dry. Drawing himself inward, he rubbed a thumb against my hand.

"Anyway, I ain't ever gonna tell on your daddy."

"I think he did it, Ben," I said. "I really do."

Saying nothing, neither one of us moved. We had a staring contest, and I thought I'd won when he closed his eyes. Instead, he pressed his mouth against mine, and it was soft. Dry and warm, too, a familiar gesture that felt strange for lingering.

I closed my eyes, just for a second, overaware of everything. My heart pulsed until it stopped on a single, captured beat, and I felt dipped in summer again, searing everywhere.

Pulling back, I swiped my lips with the back of my hand to rub in any mark he might have left behind.

"You better go home, Ben," I said.

After the warmth of his mouth, I felt cold all over and couldn't look at him. Elijah'd gotten himself killed this way.

No wonder he picked me—I was just as bad.

&

For a week, I had nightmares. I felt sick all the time, aching for everything missing, wanting to pull out my hair and grieve in loud, wrenching sobs. Any kind of penance would have helped, but I needed *things*.

I needed Collette to be my other half again, but it looked like she was never coming back. I needed Ben to be some dumb boy who threw rocks at us again, and nothing else. I needed my daddy to be innocent and Elijah to stay dead. Most of all, I needed somebody to notice I'd shattered.

Plodding through my waking hours, I did my chores automatically and tasted nothing when I ate, until I suddenly burst into tears over supper. The salt didn't improve the peas much, but Daddy finally moved.

"Sugar, what's wrong?" He pushed his plate aside and slid his chair close to mine, wrapping me up in his arms.

Surrounded by the scent of his aftershave and the warm, strong cage of his hug, I cried harder. How could I tell him anything? How could I say I was being haunted? How could I explain kissing my best friend's boyfriend?

How could I look him in the face and tell him I knew what he'd done?

My belly hitched with hiccups, and I had to fight my own throat to answer him. "I don't know."

Through my gulps and whimpers, I could hear him whispering nonsense promises, reassurances that everything would be all right, but that just made me cry harder. Nothing would ever be right again; that was one thing I knew for certain.

When I'd settled down to ragged gasps, Daddy pushed me back and reached for a napkin. He studied me, like he could read my mind, concerned as he mopped up my face. His touch was soft under my eyes but hard beneath my nose.

Balling that napkin up, he reached for another and handed it to me. "Blow your nose, baby."

I was glad he didn't hold it for me. Between honks, I apologized. "I didn't mean to ruin supper."

"We can have peas any day," he said, taking my dirty napkins and throwing them away. Turning on the tap with his wrist, he washed his hands but watched me over his shoulder. "You know you can talk to me, Iris."

"Uncle Lee gave me Mama's memory book," I said. I turned in my chair and stared at him, trying to look into him. "How come you didn't have it? How come I had to get it from him?"

Daddy slumped slightly, drying his hands on an old towel. "Because he's the only one with any sense."

"Daddy, what are you talking about?"

"I wanted to throw everything away," he said. "After her funeral, it was just too hard. Lee took the important things home instead. He thought you might want them someday."

I looked toward the living room. "Then how come you kept the couch?"

"Sofa's too heavy to throw away in a fit," Daddy said.

His shamed smile softened my heart. Already heading for the stairs, I said, "You should look."

"Iris, I . . ."

"I'll be right back." I tore up to my room and nearly broke my neck coming back down. Pushing my plate to the middle of the table, I spread the book out. I wanted him to look at it with me. I needed him to.

131

He hesitated, then leaned in, framing the book with his arm. "It's been a long time."

"You went a lot of places," I said, stopping at the camping pictures.

Daddy worked a nail under the plastic sleeve to pull out a photograph of Mama sitting on his lap by a tent. "Actually, that was Eddie Lanoux's backyard. They lived a ways out and had a good piece of land. We never brought enough matches. Half the time we ended up sneaking into the house to make supper."

I turned the book a little to get the glare of the lights off the plastic. "Did Mama take this one?"

"Yes, ma'am, and all the ones with her in them, too. She had a timer. She wouldn't let anybody else mess with her camera, not even a little." Daddy shook his head at himself and sighed. "I never told you about Katie and her pictures."

That hit a hollow place, one I wanted filled up so badly it ached. "Huh-uh."

"She said she'd have a gallery someday. Me and Eli planned to build her a darkroom. . . ." Daddy trailed off thoughtfully. "Damned if we knew what belonged in one."

Thumbing over another page, Daddy frowned at the empty spot he found, his eyes darting over the handwriting left behind in the margin. "The parish fair should have been right here."

For a moment, I kept my silence, then admitted, "I've got it up in my room. I like it."

He gazed at the empty page as if he could see the picture that belonged there, his lips twitching with an odd smile. "We all started off together, but by midnight, Nan threw Eli over for some carnie, and I'd asked your mama to marry me." A pleased glimmer colored his eyes again, and he glanced at me. "She told me no."

Clasping the edge of the table, I twisted in my chair to look up at him. "She changed her mind, though!"

"Only after she spent spring break in New Orleans." Flicking to the next page, he glanced at it briefly, then closed the memory book softly. "She'd been planning on moving there after high school. She wanted her gallery to be right on the water, and I liked Ondine just fine.

"She went for two weeks, and when she came back, she marched up to my front door and said, 'All right, Jack, what did you do to ruin my city?' And I just looked at her and said, 'I stayed here.' "

Daddy leaned his chair back, smoothing a hand over his hair. "She didn't plan on taking me back, but I think it scared her when Eli died."

I forced myself to stay still, but God, it was hard. My daddy had just told on himself.

Trying to be all nonchalant, I picked up the memory book and held it to my chest. "How do you know he's dead?"

Daddy clamped down on his memories and started to clear the table. "I guess I don't. Why don't you put that book away before it gets ruined?"

How could he mourn Elijah if he killed him? He should have looked guilty or scared or maybe both or something, but not heartbroken.

"Do you miss him?"

He looked right into me; he crackled with possibility. And then he nudged me gently. "I said go on."

"Yes, sir," I said, and stole upstairs with my thoughts.

After a couple of lonely days, Daddy tapped on my door and told me to get my shoes on. I did as I was told, but I asked, "Where are we going?"

Holding up a covered plate, Daddy said, "I'm going to play cards with Eddie, and you're making up with Collette."

In the dusk, we walked over to the Lanouxs' with an offering of thick brownies, all with nuts because that was how Daddy liked them and he wouldn't bend on that, even for me.

Shoving my hands in my pockets, I smiled up at Mr. Lanoux when he opened the door, and I asked, "Is Collette home?"

"Upstairs, peaches." Winking at me, he plucked an exposed walnut from the brownies to pop into his mouth.

Music rolled out of Collette's room, just loud enough that it was pointless to knock. Opening the door a crack, I snuck inside and closed the door by leaning on it.

She'd made a couple of changes since the last time I'd been in: she'd replaced her pink covers with wine red ones and had grown a collection of overstuffed pillows in shades of gold and bronze. The colors matched a new robe I'd never seen her wear before. She lounged on her belly in the middle of the bed, her bare feet waving in the air, stilling when she realized she wasn't alone. Looking up from a magazine, Collette let me see a brief, scathing frown, then turned back to her article. "What do you want?"

"I found out some more stuff," I said, my feet pinned in place. Sliding down to sit, I squeezed the rock in my pocket, willing Collette to look at me again. "My daddy messed up when he was talking to me about Mama."

"What, did he tell you he personally cut off Elijah's head?"

Strangled by big gulps of pride, I shrugged. "I think I was wrong about that part."

Thin magazine pages crinkled, then the bed groaned as Collette shifted to look back at me. "You think?"

I tugged my knees to my chest. "You don't have to be ugly."

Collette grabbed the edge of the bed and pulled herself down to sit on the end. Leaning forward, she curved her mouth into an icy smile, one that didn't have any humor to it at all. "You went too far, Iris. He was already your ghost. You didn't have to make your daddy kill him, too."

A flare of heat rose in my chest, threatening to become a blush. "I said I was sorry."

"No, you said you were wrong."

"Fine, I'm sorry, all right? I thought it made sense!" Then I cut myself off. "Why am I apologizing to you, anyway? You're the one who got nasty with me!"

Collette stood up, her crimson robe falling like waves all around her. "I didn't, either. You *did* lie about the witch-board! Probably none of it's true. Ben told me he threw the rock at the séance."

"He did not."

"Yeah, he did." She graced me with another cold smile.

Unsteady, I wavered. "Did he do the knocking, too?"

"I figured you made up everything else."

"I didn't, though!"

Showing off another flash of the whites of her eyes, Collette sank down to ignore me some more.

My lower lip trembled, and I bit it hard to keep it still.

"Facts are facts. Elijah really did go missing, and Daddy

said he'd died like he knew it for sure. If everybody else thinks he disappeared, and my daddy knows he died, then—"

"Don't you get it? I don't care!"

I grabbed the doorknob and hauled myself up. I'd had just about enough of her, and I was starting to get mad that I was the one apologizing. Maybe Collette did think she was right, but I thought I was, too, and that hadn't stopped *me* from saying sorry. "You used to before you went all boy-crazy!"

"At least the boys I like aren't dead!"

"At least the boys I like like me back," I snapped.

Before Collette could figure that one out, the door shoved open enough to knock me in the head.

Rooster flung himself into the room, dancing like a rodeo clown. "Y'all in trouble—we could hear you yelling downstairs!"

Grabbing Rooster by the shoulders, Collette pushed him into the hall and slammed the door. "I told you to stay out of my room!"

Instead of going away like a sensible person would have, Rooster stood in the hall and knocked on the door. He knocked loud and soft; he knocked "Twinkle, Twinkle" and belched out every *star* before starting over again.

Cutting a glance at me, Collette set her jaw. "See what you did?"

I gritted my teeth and whispered through them. I knew if I started with Collette, we'd never make up again. "I wasn't the only one yelling."

"You started it," Collette hissed, bracing her shoulder

against the door when Rooster realized knocking wasn't annoying enough and decided to bounce off it instead.

Forcing myself to give up just a little, I helped her lean against the door. "We both started it. I'm just trying to finish it."

"I see London, I see—"

Rooster cut off with a yelp when heavy footsteps came down the hall. The doorknob jiggled again, and me and Collette jumped back to let her mama in.

Already shaking her head, Mrs. Lanoux crossed her arms over her chest. "Do I even want to know?"

I didn't say anything. Collette looked me over, then spread her hands out helplessly. "We were just doing a play, and dummy Rooster wouldn't leave us alone."

Weary, Mrs. Lanoux craned down the hall, ignoring us for a minute to yell out a warning. "Boy, get in there and take your bath like I told you to!" Answered by a thump, then the sound of running water, Mrs. Lanoux turned to us again. "Try to keep it down to a dull roar."

"We will," Collette said, all but pushing her mama into the hall and closing the door on her. Whipping around to face me, she lifted her chin. "You owe me."

Considering she had kept us both out of trouble, not just me, I didn't see how. But I wasn't gonna argue with the offering of a peace branch.

Pulling my hands from my pockets, I looked at her. "Do you really not care anymore?"

Collette rolled her shoulders in a great shrug, her robe shimmering all the way down her arms. "I don't know. What did you find out?"

"Well, for one, Miss Nan lied to us."

The dark sparkle came back to Collette's eyes, both brows rising until they disappeared beneath her curls. "About what?"

I opened the door for a minute, listening for voices around the house. Rooster warbled from the bathroom, and after a minute, I heard my daddy laughing downstairs. Comfortable that they wouldn't notice us again, I locked the door and nodded at Collette's radio.

"Turn that up."

Drowned out by the music, I told her my plan.

chapter thirteen

&

We jimmied the screen loose and jumped off the sloped roof, carrying our shoes to keep from making too much noise. The trees attacked us, their gnarled twig fingers reaching out to snatch our hair, and we tripped more than once on the uneven ground.

I felt giddy and Collette must have, too, because she couldn't stop giggling. It was our best escape ever. When we poured into Ben's backyard, she turned to me with a drunken smile. "I can't believe we just snuck out like that."

"Me either," I said, trying to keep myself from bouncing.

The way I figured it, we had about a half hour before anybody came looking for us. The CDs played just loud enough to hide the emptiness of Collette's room, and the locked door would keep Rooster from barging in to find out otherwise.

I loved my plan; I felt like a genius.

Since we were being wicked anyway, we threw pebbles at Ben's window instead of going to the front door. He didn't have to be in for his curfew for another couple of hours, but what good was sneaking out without acting up a little?

Raising his screen, Ben leaned out to squint at us. "What are y'all doing?"

"Come down and we'll tell you," Collette said, putting her hands on her hips. She smiled up at him, jutting one hip out and tilting her head.

Ben ducked inside. One invasion must have been enough for him, because he popped out the back door, then looked up at his window in relief. "Where y'all at?"

"We're fine," Collette purred. She half yanked my arm off and put me on display. "Guess what."

"What?" Ben hunched over, his hands searching for pockets his sweatpants didn't have.

Ben had so much on his mind—his mama, his daddy, what he and his brother had done—I felt guilty for piling a murder on his conscience, too. I hoped taking it back would make things better. A little, anyway.

"I was wrong about my daddy, Ben." I nodded, sincere. "He knew Elijah died, but he didn't kill him."

And I think it did help. All at once, Ben seemed to grow taller. His back straightened, and a smile curved the corners of his mouth. "Well, that's good to know."

I nodded. "Yeah. So I don't know exactly what happened, but he didn't do it. And"—I nearly knocked myself over when I waved my hand too hard—"Miss Nan lied. She and Elijah broke up before Easter."

"They could've gotten back together," Collette said, trying to be fair. That didn't last long, though; she took a breath and then said, "But still, she didn't say anything to us about running around with a carnie. I mean, she dumped him right there at the fair!"

Rocking back on his heels, Ben considered it. "Maybe Miss Nan killed him and your daddy found out."

That didn't feel right to me, and I shook my head. "But then he woulda looked for him. His body, I mean. Or told on her, at least."

"Oh, I know!" Collette drew a map in the air, trying to put people into position to illustrate her point. "Maybe Elijah ran away and got a new identity, then found out he was dying and wrote a goodbye note!"

Ben kicked at the dirt, furrowing his brows. "But why wouldn't he tell his mama that?"

Snorting, Collette flipped her hair over her shoulder. "Uh, because she's crazy?"

The wind picked up, and I had to curve my hands against my face to keep my hair from my eyes. I looked into the dark, expecting to see somebody watching us. Nobody was there.

"He could have killed himself," I said. "I think I'd know it if y'all wanted to go off and die somewhere, so maybe Elijah's friends did, too. I wouldn't want to go looking and find you dead, you know?"

Collette shuffled from foot to foot, giving my theory a moment of life before killing it. "I think he had a secret identity and cancer."

Wincing, Ben shrugged. "Maybe."

Sure of herself, Collette added, "We still don't know why he was in the hospital."

A glow of white light poured onto the lawn, and Ben's

mama stepped onto the porch. She was only a shadow, but I could see the wisps of dark hair that escaped her scarf to swirl around her head. "Wind it up, baby."

"Yes, ma'am," Ben said, caught having a mama who still called him pet names in public. Lowering his voice, he stepped closer. "You wanna go to the cemetery tomorrow and we can work on this some more?"

"We'll be there." Collette lingered like she wanted to stay behind for a private minute, but then she looked me over and started toward the woods. "I wonder if we can get old medical records at the library?"

Starting to follow Collette, I told her I thought medical records stayed private forever, and then stopped at the tree line. "I forgot to ask Ben something. I'll be right back," I said, ignoring her bothered frown. I caught him right before he closed the door.

Ben put his shoulder between the door and the frame, half inside, half out. Shadows played on his brow. "What's wrong?"

Tugging on the hem of my shirt, I glanced over my shoulder at Collette. "Did you throw that rock when you were at my house?"

Incredibly quiet, Ben smiled uncomfortably and looked away. "I didn't mean to hit the glass. That was an accident."

A sigh rolled out of me. "What about the knocks?"

"No, ma'am," he said, holding both hands up to swear his innocence. "That wasn't me."

Mindful that Ben wasn't the only one to make things up about Elijah, I summoned as much generosity as I could. "Just don't do anything else like that, all right?"

"I won't." He raised a hand to his collar but dropped it right away. I guess he remembered he was too old to cross his heart and hope to die. "I'm sorry you got hurt."

Bouncing down the steps before he got too close to me, I waved off his apology with a good, queenly smile. "I got better, didn't I?"

I didn't wait to see him agree; instead, I ran to catch up with Collette. It was a short run through the darkened woods, and the shadows were too familiar to scare us.

When we saw the lights coming from Collette's house, she finally turned to me. "What did you want to ask Ben?"

I didn't get a chance to answer. Our daddies were standing at the back door, and neither one wore a smile.

&

"I don't understand you, Iris."

"Nobody said we couldn't leave," I mumbled. He hadn't said a word to me the whole walk home.

The air conditioner kicked on in our living room. Just knowing Daddy was mad thickened the air in the house. I tried to slip upstairs silently, like he might not notice my leaving if I was quiet enough.

"Where do you think you're going?"

Stiffening, I stopped at the doorway, but I didn't turn around. I didn't want to see the hangdog look on his face.

"Sit down." I could hear the frown in his voice, and I dragged my feet on my way to the table. I kept my attention on the patterns in the wood as I sat playing with my fingers, waiting for my sentence.

Clearing his throat, Daddy sat back. "You're going to

stop running around in the middle of the night. I don't care how grown you think you are; you're not."

"Daddy."

"Don't 'Daddy' me," he said. He sounded tired and frustrated, and he kept wiping the same clean spot on the table over and over. "I don't know what's gotten into you this summer, but it's going to stop."

"I'm just the same!"

Daddy whipped his head up. "Is it that Duvall boy?"

My cheeks burned. "What? No! Why would you even think that?"

Closing his eyes for a second, he took a breath, then looked me right in the eye. As plain as he could be, he said, "Then you tell me what I'm supposed to think."

"Ben's a good person!" Jumping up from my chair, I knocked it over in my scramble toward the stairs. "Collette's got dibs, anyway."

He called after me, but I ran as fast as I could and threw myself into my room. Right then, I hated everybody and everything, and when I found a pyramid of brand-new rocks in the middle of my bed, I cracked. Snatching them up, I screamed at Elijah to leave me alone, too. Glass sparkled like snow, and it was so pretty that it didn't occur to me I shouldn't have broken my window like that.

Footsteps pounded up the stairs, and my door flew open. Daddy towered there, his face twisted up, his expression between furious and terrified. In slow motion, I watched him take in the broken window, then me, too stunned to speak, let alone yell.

Letting the rest of the rocks tumble from my hands, I sat

down hard on the end of my bed, vomiting up sudden sobs that hurt all the way from my belly to my throat.

Afraid to move, I sat there stiff as I could and said between gasps, "Elijah made me, Daddy. He made me do it."

&

Where I lived, people who went crazy were allowed to with respect. We didn't see psychiatrists, we didn't take happy pills, and we didn't go to the state hospital unless we did something so wild nobody knew how to handle it.

All I'd done was talk out of my head some, so Daddy decided, like most people would, that I should talk to our priest. He got me up early and told me to put on church clothes. It was all right to go crazy in Ondine, but you had to look decent while you were doing it.

Father Rey's office smelled like fried fish. It was a tiny little room, with plaster walls decorated in pretty blue-caped-Mary pictures and lots and lots of books. From where I sat, I could make out a collection of science-fiction novels on a bottom shelf.

It wasn't a real convenient time to lose my mind. My grumbling stomach turned sour, and I glowered because Collette would have a chance to talk Ben into her stupid sick-and-dying idea before I even got to argue my side.

Finally, the door opened and Father Rey came in. Clasping his hands together as he sat, Father Rey smiled at me, posed to listen and understand. "I think we both know why you're here, Miss Iris, so why don't you tell me what's on your mind?"

"I'm just having a bad summer," I said, crossing my ankles, then freeing them to keep my attention from wandering toward the window. "My best friend went all funny, and my daddy thinks I'm running around with boys and I'm not. That's all."

Father Rey rubbed his thumbs together, his soft skin whispering with each brush, and his smile never faltered. "Well, we can talk about that, but why don't you tell me why you think Elijah Landry's haunting you?"

My throat turning dry, I shifted in my chair uncomfortably. I'd go right to hell for lying to a priest, so I mumbled an "I don't know" and hoped that would be enough.

"Your father's concerned," Father Rey said, his smile serious. "And so am I. I'm worried about your mind, but I'm worried about your soul, too."

Something felt wrong, like Father Rey knew more than he should have, so I hedged. "I don't know why I said what I did last night. I was just mad."

Father Rey reclasped his hands, studying my face. "And what about the Ouija board? All the time you're spending in the cemetery?"

A chill swept through me, and I glanced to the door instead of answering. I wanted to poke my fingers into Daddy's brain and find out exactly what he'd told Father Rey and how he'd known what to tell him.

"You know, Iris, an imagination is a wonderful thing to have." Father Rey's smile came back briefly, like that proved it was okay for me to think all kinds of things. "But you have to understand that the dead are in God's hands. The only way you can talk to them is through prayer."

I knew Father Rey meant what he said, but my whole

summer told me he was wrong. "Yeah, but they don't answer back when you pray."

Father Rey wrapped his hands around the arms of his chair, lifting it to slide closer to me. "They don't answer at all, Iris. They're beyond this world, and any answer you get is a lie. All the pain you've suffered trying to follow that path, that was a warning from God."

The cold dug down a little deeper, starting to ache in my joints. "I don't know what you mean."

Concern wrinkled his brow, and he pressed two fingers to his temple, offering examples when I didn't say anything. "You got a sunburn waiting for him in the cemetery, didn't you? And you had an upsetting encounter with Mrs. Landry? I understand you've been fighting with your best friend over this."

Inside, my body stopped. Daddy knew about Old Mrs. Landry and the fights I got in with Collette, but as far as he knew, I got the sunburn playing outside. My heart didn't beat, and I didn't draw a breath. Betrayal stole my voice away.

Uncle Lee had told on me.

I thought I could trust him, but he'd tattled everything to Daddy. I swore to myself I'd never trust him again.

Pressing my teeth together until I felt pressure behind my eyes, I stared at the priest. "People get in fights all the time."

Father Rey sighed, the very picture of tried patience. As interesting as he was to look at, I decided right then I didn't like him. He tried too hard to be friendly.

"God gives us signs every day to tell us if we're on the right path, Iris, and I'm afraid you're not."

"Well, I'm done with it, anyway." Lifting my chin, I

made as if to stand up, meaning to sound bored. I think it came out whiny, but I didn't care. "Are we done?"

Father Rey stood up slowly, then waited for me to join him. Putting a hand on my shoulder, he walked me toward the door. "I want you to think about our talk in earnest. Pray about it and examine yourself. I think with enough reflection, you'll realize what God's been trying to tell you all along."

I just nodded and slipped to the back of the church to light a candle for Mama.

I could admit I was crazy, but I'd prove to them I'd been listening to Elijah all along. I just didn't know how yet.

&

After I changed out of my church clothes, I went downstairs and told Daddy I was leaving. Almost businesslike, I stood at his chair to give him my schedule. He had other ideas.

He rubbed his hands against the back of his jeans. "Windows don't grow on trees, and you've got a lot of work to do to pay for a new one."

It didn't get much plainer than that. I stomped upstairs to change into my work jeans, the ones spattered with paint and permanently grass-stained at the knees.

I kicked my bed on purpose and bumped my elbows against the walls as I stormed downstairs again. He could make me a slave all he wanted, but he couldn't make me work hard or cheerfully.

Parking me in the vegetable patch, Daddy handed me a spade and set me to weeding while he pulled out clippers to prune back our bushes.

I took my time getting down in the dirt. Then I plucked weeds one at a time, as slow as I could. The sun beat down on my back, soaking into my dark blue T-shirt and drawing an instant sweat to my skin. I figured I'd die of heatstroke in Daddy's prison camp; when I asked if I could get a drink of water, he just shot me an ugly look.

My hands sank into the garden. I dug in deep to yank out a weed with broad, fuzzy leaves and little thorns on the stem. Cool and hard beneath a bed of earth, the roots felt like bones, and I shuddered as I worked between them to yank them out.

I planted my knees hard on the ground and pulled, sort of convinced I'd pull out a skeleton or a plant that went all the way to China. Something snapped and I ended up flat on my back, a spray of dirt raining on my face.

A cool shadow fell on me, and when I opened my eyes, I saw someone standing over me. It was Ben, I was sure of it, until I heard his voice.

"Where y'at, Iris?"

I heaved myself to my feet. Elijah's shadow was already gone, but his voice lingered. My heart pounded, beating my ribs so hard my chest ached. I turned to try to catch a glimpse of him. I saw nothing but my yard and my daddy working in it.

Tossing the pricker bush aside, I delved into the vegetable patch again. Just when I'd settled down, I felt a warm breath against my ear.

I didn't dare move, though I did manage a whisper. "Quit messing with me, Elijah."

A cold touch swept up the back of my neck. "You found me where I'm sleeping," Elijah said, his voice low.

149

It happened again: that feeling like I'd been invaded. Unwelcome hands clasped my shoulders. Flinging off the sensation, I crossed myself and yelled to Daddy I was getting a drink whether he wanted me to or not, then ran into the house. I don't know if it was the crossing or the door slamming, but once I was inside, I felt alone again, and I said a little prayer of thanks for that.

chapter fourteen

&

Daddy had an awful surprise for me when he went back
to work. Leaving me to fill his thermos while he answered
the door, he let Mrs. Thacker in and folded a thin stack of
bills in her worn hand. Telling her that I'd been acting up,
he warned her to check on me after I went to bed. I couldn't
go out; nobody could come in, either.

As soon as Daddy left, Mrs. Thacker turned on the television and smiled at me with her yellow, craggy teeth. "Did
you miss me?"

I tugged my T-shirt over my knees and stared at the TV,
offering up a noise that could have been yes or no, depend-
ing on how generous her hearing was that night.

"Tell me about your summer," she said.

Curling my toes into the couch, I refused to look over.
"It's been all right."

"Oh, but didn't the police come?" Mrs. Thacker tried to

make it sound innocent, like maybe she wasn't sure if it had been my house or some other house on the street, but I knew better. She ate gossip like candy; she probably knew exactly how many rocks we'd found in my room and how many Old Mrs. Landry claimed I'd thrown at her windows.

When I didn't answer, Mrs. Thacker patted the arm of the chair with her dry hand. Leaning her head back, she sighed. "If your daddy had any sense, he'd take a new wife."

"He don't need a wife," I said sullenly.

"It's my opinion," Mrs. Thacker said, working into a full chorus of croaks, "that a man can't handle a child on his own. They turn out funny without a mother's touch."

I burrowed into the couch; I wanted to stick cotton in my ears and drown her out. "In my opinion, we turn out just fine."

"Look at poor Lee, living in sin with that man in Baton Rouge." Mrs. Thacker ignored me, her finger bobbing like a metronome. "He wouldn't be like that if your granny had lived."

My mouth burned. I wanted to shout at her, *Shut up, shut up, shut up!*

I wanted to, but I couldn't. I had to mind. I had to be good enough to get rid of her, for good. Reaching for the remote, I said, "I can't hear the TV."

Not that Mrs. Thacker cared. She found a special frequency that went right into my brain. No matter how hard I tried to ignore her, her voice came through. She went on about my daddy and about what a shame it was my mama had died so young, on and on until I was sick with it. My eyes dried out as I watched the clock, blue digital numbers creeping upward somehow slower than a minute at a time.

"... got laid up at the hospital. Of course, with that mama of his, he coulda had a whole boxful of reasons for doing something so foolish."

I peeked around my arm at her, trying to decide if I wanted her to repeat that or not. It sounded like she was talking about Elijah, but she could have been talking about her Henry and his bullfighting days for all I knew. Forcing myself to sound disinterested, I leaned back in the couch. "What'd he go for, anyway?"

"Now you're interested," Mrs. Thacker said with a snide smile. "Nobody likes a gossip, Iris."

She should know, I thought.

Mrs. Thacker thumped my arm waving her hand in a little circle between us, binding us to a secret. "Delinda Potts used to come in twice a week to clean because Babette always was too precious to do it herself. According to her, that boy swallowed a whole bottle of aspirin and had to have his stomach pumped."

I stared at her. "Why'd he do something like that?"

"Haven't you been listening? Love! It's either love or money, and he wasn't old enough to worry about money." Mrs. Thacker dropped back in the recliner, cackling again. "It's a good thing you look like your daddy, or we would have wondered."

I knew she wanted me to ask more, but I'd heard everything I wanted to. Pulling my legs out of my shirt, I peeled myself off the couch with a fake yawn. "I better go to bed."

With a frown, Mrs. Thacker turned to watch me go,

raising her voice to call after me, "Don't you lock your door; I'm going to be checking on you."

As soon as I got the phone from Daddy's room, I locked myself up tight anyway and shoved a book under the door just to make sure she couldn't walk in unannounced. I had a notion to pour my box of marbles in the hallway as a guarantee, but a quick, vivid image of Mrs. Thacker lying at the bottom of the stairs, her head twisted the wrong way, turned me off that. I didn't like her, but I didn't want to kill her.

&

Beneath a stack of covers, I made myself small as I picked up the phone and dialed. After Collette got done hassling me for missing our date at the cemetery, she settled in to listen. She made soft, surprised sounds as I talked, and I could practically hear her nod over the line. I kept my latest Elijah sightings to myself, though. I wanted to work out his riddle on my own.

"You ought to tell your daddy what she said about your family." For some reason, Collette had jumped back all the way to the beginning instead of saying anything about my new evidence. "That woman's mean as a scorpion."

It felt good to have her on my side again, and I nodded. "She is. And she's got a nasty mouth for an old lady."

"They ought to lock her and Old Mrs. Landry in a cage together. They could sting each other to death."

"You think she's lying, though? About Elijah, I mean. I know she was lying about my mama." I popped my arm out of the covers, trying to make a little hole for fresh air.

"I don't know." Collette hummed softly, then added, "Swallowing pills doesn't sound like something a boy would do. A boy would want a gun, I'd think."

I rolled Collette's point over in my head. It sounded right, and I couldn't argue it, but then I remembered something. "Miss Nan said he wasn't allowed to go hunting, though. If he didn't have a gun, he might take pills."

"Well, Miss Nan said he wasn't allowed to have a girl-friend, but there she was," Collette said.

Annoyed, I frowned. "You can sneak and have a girl-friend. How do you sneak and have a gun? I think Mrs. Thacker's right."

Another hum crackled over the line. "We should ask Ben; he'd know."

Throwing the covers off my head, I swabbed the sweat from my face and let loose on her. "He wouldn't know any better than you would, and I asked you. You can think just fine without running to Ben to ask if it's all right, you know."

"I know I can, but he's a boy, so he would know about boys."

"He knows about himself, and that's it!" Sliding out of bed, I stalked over to turn up the box fan. Its whine filled my room, white noise that cleared my head like cool water. "I think we're about done playing magic, Collette."

Collette answered with a gasp that sounded like a hiccup. "You're the most jealous thing I've ever seen, Iris."

"Maybe I am, but some stuff was just ours—the spellbook and all that. But it's not anymore." Tempering myself, I leaned against the wall. "I'm not saying don't be my friend."

"Yes you are, too."

I slumped against the wall and sighed. "If that's what you want to think, I can't stop you." I wasn't mad anymore, just tired. "I'll be here if you want to watch movies or listen to music or talk about anything, but I'm done acting like we have powers. We don't; we never did."

"You just want to keep Elijah to yourself." Collette's voice sounded thin and wet, like she'd started crying. "You go on ahead and see if I care, because I don't."

Emptied of everything, I sat at my desk, curling one arm into a pillow so I could rest my head. "Nobody said you had to. I'm going to bed now, Collette."

She sniffled, the line going fuzzy, then clear again. After using that moment to calm down, Collette tried to put on her best queen voice. It didn't work; she didn't sound chilly or regal or even hard—she just sounded sad. "Well, then good night."

"I'll talk to you later," I said, then hung up the phone. I sat there for a long time, rearranging things on my desk before going back to bed.

When I told Collette I'd talk to her later, I meant it. I didn't know how to be a person without my best friend; Collette knew me from the inside, all my dumb details and the good ones, too.

I had to believe she'd still like me without our spells and swords. I had to believe we were more than make-believe.

&

Elijah walked through my bedroom door and started pulling books from the shelves. His hair looked mossy, his skin mint green and mottled, but his mouth was red as an apple.

Pages flapped when he tossed books over his shoulder. Carefully, he pulled the prayer book Daddy had given me for my First Communion from the shelf and sniffed it. I liked to do that, too; it was bound in white leather, and the pages were edged in gold.

Elijah stroked it for a minute, but instead of just dumping it over his shoulder like the rest, he wound up and threw it hard. It turned into a rock and shattered my window. Still, he didn't seem to enjoy destroying my things; he frowned and thumped the wall, like he expected it to open or something.

Unsure if this was a dream, I didn't try to move, but I shuddered when he turned to shake out my desk. He only wore half a face; the other side was bone, gray and dirty, barely held together. His bright lips stopped exactly in the middle, and I could see a black tongue filling his mouth.

"Don't ask me where I'm at," I said, wrapping the covers around me tight. "You already know."

His face melted from green to gold again, from half to whole again, a feathered sweep of hair falling into his eyes. When he leaned back, his jersey shirt pulled tight across his shoulders, showing off fine, sculpted muscles beneath. "You already know," he echoed.

Shivering, I tried to rearrange the blankets to cover me, but I couldn't get warm. Rocks filled my bed. Breath frosting in the air, I shook my head. "That's what I said."

"You already know," he repeated, and reached to grab something off my desk. He threw my spellbook toward me, and its white pages rose and fell like a bird's wings before it landed silently in my lap.

The book flipped over and spread itself open. I closed it and frowned when it popped open again. A red drop splattered in the middle of the page, and I reached up to scrub at my nose as the blood smear crawled across the page and formed neat block letters.

You found me where I'm sleeping.

Reading the blood note, I held both hands against my nose, swallowing the iron tang sliding down my throat. I lifted my head to tell Elijah I still didn't know what he meant by that, but he was gone.

&

I threw the covers off when an awful flash of heat swept over me. Humid night air choked me as I struggled free from the tangle of sheets around my ankles. Just to make sure I'd been dreaming, I looked up to find my room the way it had been when I fell asleep.

Outside my window, angry clouds blotted out the moon. I felt the static hum of a coming storm in everything I touched, and fighting a low, sick feeling in my stomach, I rolled out of bed. I needed to get the fan out of the window before the rain came.

As I reached for the fan, something loomed behind me, something that made the hair stand up on the back of my neck. More stupid than brave, I looked over my shoulder and almost lost my legs from under me.

A black pool of blood stained my sheets, and a single rock fell from nowhere. Uneasy, I looked down and saw blood on my legs. I could smell it, a dead, heavy scent that turned my stomach. I backed toward the door, touching myself, trying to find where I'd been cut.

Another rock fell, sounding almost hollow as it rolled off the bed and onto the floor. I didn't know if it was the storm or something else, but papers rustled on my desk, and as I reached blindly for the doorknob, I watched my drawer work itself open.

I screamed when the drawer exploded out, showering my room with crayons and books and pictures and every other little thing I'd tucked away in there.

My door wouldn't open. I ducked when my spellbook slammed against the wall beside my head. Struggling for another breath I screamed again. Mrs. Thacker was about the worst babysitter in the world if she couldn't hear this.

I damned her and the television set blaring downstairs. I damned Daddy for working nights, and Mama for driving in the rain, and Collette for growing up, and Ben for coming between us. I damned them for leaving me all alone with this when it wasn't a dream.

The storm in my room raged for a second; then suddenly the phone rang and everything stopped. Pens and boxes and books began raining down like hail again as I dropped to my hands and knees, crawling through the mess to get to the phone.

"Collette," I whispered, panicking when a warm, wet stream trickled from my nose. I swabbed at it, relieved that it was snot instead of blood.

The line crackled with soft static, and then a voice murmured, "Where y'at, Iris?"

I threw the phone and scrambled to my feet. With both

hands, I yanked at my bedroom door, but it stuck fast. I tore around, searching for a way to escape, and my gaze landed on the window. I pulled the fan free, pushed my screen out, and slung my leg outside.

My bedroom opened onto nothing. Clinging to the sill, I kept telling myself it wasn't far to the ground; all I had to do was let go. My fingers didn't care; they dug in hard, and I dangled there with the wind clawing at me until a bright crack of lightning scared me into letting go.

The ground rushed up under me, shoving the air from my lungs when we collided. Eyes crossing, arms spread out wide, I watched the sky go blurry, then sharp above me.

All I wanted was to go to sleep, but spatters of rain hit my face. Those cold little drops jerked me sensible again, and suddenly I knew.

chapter fifteen

&

With Daddy's tire iron in one hand, I staggered through the cemetery. The skies split with sheets of cold rain. I felt like I'd sunk into an ice bath; hard, jolting shivers twisted me off balance.

There weren't any lights at the graveyard, so I made my way by memory and luck. Bad luck, mostly, because I stumbled into low stones that bit my shins, and I nearly fell into the black iron fence that surrounded one of the family plots. Pushing myself away from that, I shuddered when lightning lit up the spikes I'd barely missed.

The Claibornes' crypts lay farther in than I thought. The white limestone seemed to glow, collecting the brightness of the lightning and holding on to it when the flashes faded. Circling Cecily, I curved a hand on my brow to hold off the rain and examined the seam that ran between the top of the slab and the crypt.

Finding a slightly chipped spot, I forced Daddy's tire iron between the crypt and the slab and pushed hard. The muscles in my arms screamed, threatening to snap, but I didn't stop. Grinding my teeth, I pushed again, the ache radiating into my shoulders, then down my back, but the slab wouldn't move.

I kept at it anyway; then my hands slipped and I crashed headfirst into the stone. Sliding to my knees in the mud, I rubbed the throbbing goose egg rising on my forehead. The pain jangled around in my head, throbbing until my brain felt too big for my skull.

The stone pulled my hair, yanking strands of it out as I struggled to my feet again. Shaking off the pain, I told myself those little stings meant nothing. I dried my hands on my shirt and shoved the tire iron back into the crack.

Twisting for leverage, I fought the grave as hard as I could. The iron felt dangerous; my hands were cold on the slick metal, and the nub end of the iron pressed into my chest. Even though it was blunt I could imagine impaling myself on it, and I shuddered. But I had to keep going.

The crypt's soft stone ground each time I pried, sending a nasty, bone-crunching sensation up the metal that made me want to boil my hands in bleach. After another failed push that sent me off my feet again, I sat there for a minute and just stared.

Rain poured down my face, and a strange, warm numbness started through me. It began at my hands and flooded my body with each pulse until I stepped out of my icy skin, hot-blooded and strong

Instead of pushing, I laced my hands together as tight as I could and looped them around the iron. I hung from it, bouncing to use all my weight. Something gave, and for a minute, I thought the iron had bent; if I wasn't already in trouble, I would have been for destroying Daddy's tools, but the iron was fine.

Cecily's slab lifted just a tiny bit, a thin black line that encouraged me to push harder. The gap spread by tiny inches, and I felt like my head might pop from the strain, but I didn't stop.

I dropped my full weight hard on the iron and pushed the stone just enough to set it askew. As soon as I saw that tiny patch of space, I dropped the tire iron and darted to the other side of the crypt, shoving on one corner, then ducking back around to push the other. The stone rubbed my hands raw, but I couldn't quit; I was almost there.

A blinding light flashed in my face, and I stopped just long enough to look into it. From the road, I saw the shadow of a car and a man climbing out of it. The police.

I should have run, but I pushed harder instead, beating the slab with my hands, urged on by the man yelling at me to stop, and with a final, great shove, the slab teetered on the edge of the crypt, then fell. It broke into three pieces, waxy, irregular breaks that seemed unreal.

I climbed up the side of Cecily's grave, desperate to get a look inside. Even without the lightning, I recognized pieces of the jersey shirt, black sleeves and gray body, rotten through in places.

Trying not to gag on the smell that rolled up, I made myself look where Elijah's eyes should have been. From then to forever, I knew who carried the grave lanterns— long-dead boys with half a face, soft and green with moss.

A thin length of rope lay in a coil beside his head. It must have been white once; it was the kind we used to hang laundry in the backyard, but it had turned black.

Footsteps rushed up behind me, but I held on tight to the grave. Elijah's body was a horrible thing to look at, but I couldn't close my eyes. It was real; he was real; the whole summer was real.

I'd found him where he was sleeping, the first place I'd seen him, him and his jersey shirt, him and his torn jeans. Nobody in their right mind could believe Mrs. Cecily Claiborne had been put to rest in clothes like that.

Right before the sheriff yanked me down, I saw an old canvas bag split open at Elijah's feet. River rocks poured out of it in a heap, all of them smooth and flat just like the one in my pocket, and that was when I started to cry.

$\mathcal{C}\!\mathcal{S}$

The police didn't come to my house that time; Daddy had to come to them. A nice lady deputy had given me a cup of tea and a dry blanket to wrap around my shoulders, and when I shared an embarrassed whisper with her, she took me to the bathroom and gave me a quarter for the tampon machine.

After that, she left me alone in a big green room that smelled like medicine. I huddled in a hard plastic chair, staring at myself in a wall-length mirror. The door had a window in it, and every so often, someone would peek through it, like I was a new panda bear at the zoo.

I'd heard them buzzing, talking about me as one of the two deputies who'd shown up at the graveyard brought me in. The other one stayed behind, because after I quit fighting and screaming, I convinced them to look inside Cecily's crypt.

I enjoyed watching their faces go blank when they shone their flashlights inside, because I got the impression they just wanted to prove me wrong so I'd shut up and go quietly. As the deputy walked me to the car, I told him the body was Elijah Landry's, but I don't think he believed me.

When the door finally opened, a woman I didn't recognize walked in. She wasn't a police officer; she wore a navy blue suit that looked nice with her frosty blond hair, and she carried a thick briefcase that she swung to slide onto the table.

Right behind her came Daddy, still in his work shirt and looking so ragged I expected him to fall down from exhaustion. "This is Billie Jo Camp, Iris. She's your lawyer."

"Did anyone try to make you talk about what happened tonight?" Billie Jo asked, snapping open the latches on her briefcase. She had stacks and stacks of folders in there, and she dug through them until she found one that was almost empty.

I shook my head. Actually, I'd been waiting for somebody to talk to me so I could explain who I'd found, but after the lady deputy left, I'd been by myself the whole time. "No, ma'am."

Waving a pen at my face before uncapping it, she squinted down at me. "Did they do that to you?"

Looking into the mirror, I smiled weakly. My skin had turned papery gray, which showed off the bruise on my forehead. "No, ma'am, I fell."

The folder went back in her briefcase, and she snapped

the lid shut. With a pointed look, she said, "You stay put," like I had a choice about it, and walked out, her heels clacking on the floor.

Daddy sank into the chair across from me and folded his hands on the table. He kept his head low; all I could see of him was the part in his hair and just how many silver strands had threaded in with the dark.

When he looked up, his face was dry, but a faint shade of red rimmed his eyes. I had never seen my daddy cry. Seeing how torn he was made my heart ache.

He swallowed and swiped at his mouth, shaking his head slowly. "What did I do wrong, Iris?"

"Nothing!" I reached across the table for his hand, but he didn't stretch his fingers to meet mine. I covered his fist anyway, thinking I should feel guilty then, but instead I felt relieved. It was over, and I wouldn't disappoint him anymore. "I just had to find him, Daddy, and now I'm done. I promise."

Working a hand free, he plastered it against his forehead, like his head had grown too heavy to stay up on its own. We just sat there in silence until Billie Jo came back to say we could go home.

&

Daddy took his vacation to stay home with me. We kept our curtains closed and the doors locked, because the morning after I found Elijah, I was a headline.

I was *Local Girl Destroys Historic Grave, Finds Evidence of Murder?* The way they wrote it made me want to laugh. I kept that to myself when I saw the look on Daddy's face.

He didn't just throw the paper away; he tore it in pieces first and jammed it all the way down in the garbage. He sent Collette away when she came to the door, too. We were locked in and staying put until my court date.

Billie Jo said I'd probably get community service, but that changed after the autopsy on Wednesday. That day's paper finally told the world what I'd been insisting all along: I'd found Elijah Landry. A discovery like that, even though I'd been caught desecrating a grave, might mean I'd just get a fine. I wondered how many weeds I'd have to pull to pay for that.

The paperboy shoved our copy through the mail slot, so I got to read it while Daddy was in the shower. I shivered when they talked about me without really talking about me—I wasn't grown, so they couldn't use my name.

The story said the police planned to open the investigation again, and I snorted when I read that Deputy Wood claimed he had known the body would be found eventually. For four pages, the *Citizen* detailed the disappearance and the mystery and speculated on how Elijah had ended up sleeping with Cecily and how I'd come to find him.

Since Billie Jo did all my talking for me, and all she told anybody was "No comment," the newspaper reporters made up wild stories instead. I didn't care, because I knew the truth.

Instead of being embarrassed, I found it interesting to have people camped out on our street, waiting for us to come outside. Daddy chased them off the lawn, but the news vans just parked farther away, the people that came with them milling around like hungry dogs.

On the fifth day, the headlines turned to Old Mrs. Landry. She swore the autopsy was wrong——God had taken her boy into heaven, body and all. That thing in the Claiborne crypt, it was a lie, maybe a demon, but definitely not Elijah.

That was the day my daddy sat me at the kitchen table to go over paperwork. I had a lot of it, too.

Technically, I was arrested. They only let me go home because Daddy promised to keep me under his thumb. I had a court date the next month and an appointment with a psychiatrist that Friday. No more Father Rey; I celebrated that quietly by myself.

With a cramp in my hand from signing papers I didn't understand, I slumped on the table in relief when the doorbell rang. Daddy wouldn't answer it, but he would at least get up to tell them to go away, which gave me a minute to breathe.

Lying my head in my arms, I frowned when I heard soft conversation at the door instead of a curt goodbye. I leaned back in my chair, frowning when Mr. Lanoux and two strange men in suits walked in. Collette's daddy looked tired, with dark circles beneath his eyes, and he edged closer to Daddy, like he wanted distance between them and the other two men.

Both in brown, the men talked low, so I couldn't make the words out. When they put their hands in their pockets, I saw badges on their belts.

Slowly, I pushed my chair back and wandered to the kitchen door. "Daddy?"

Daddy looked back at me, blank and calm. "Go on upstairs, Iris."

I knew better than to argue with him. I took my time going up, though, and I stopped three steps from the top to sit and listen.

The detectives had musical voices, rolling like water, with upstate accents that made me wonder how they'd ended up in Ondine. Mr. Lanoux hadn't said a thing, that I could tell.

"I can make some coffee," Daddy said, his voice moving from the living room toward the kitchen. The detectives said that wasn't necessary, their footsteps following Daddy's.

Sliding down one stair, I strained to hear. Billie Jo had told us to keep our mouths shut, because that was our right. I didn't understand why Daddy let the police in, let alone why he'd offered them coffee.

One detective sounded bored, the sound of flipping paper punctuating his words. "We'd just like to ask you a few questions about the Landry boy."

My eyes went wide, and I slid down another step. I knew Daddy knew things, stories he'd never tell me, secrets he planned to always keep, but if the police asked, he had to tell the truth.

A second later, worry took over my curiosity. Daddy had known Elijah was dead all along. It came to me just then that I still didn't know how. If he'd done something. If he'd seen something.

Panic squeezed me; my thoughts ran fast and hot. The newspaper said *murder* over and over. No matter my visions, no matter what I knew in my bones, my daddy had known Elijah was dead, and everybody was calling it murder.

A cry caught in my throat. Because of me, my daddy could go to jail.

Kitchen chairs scraped, cutting the silence, and after a long time, Daddy cleared his throat. "We didn't mean any harm. We were young and stupid then, and I reckon we're old and stupid now."

My breath faltered. Daddy was going to confess something, something horrible Mr. Lanoux knew about. Snuffling on tears, I missed some of it but shut myself up in time to hear Daddy finish another sentence.

"We were trying to help a friend, sir. That's all."

"Well, you can see how we've got a problem, Mr. Rhame," one of the men said. The other one coughed like he wanted to call Daddy a liar but didn't dare out loud.

The chairs squeaked again, and I heard them heading for the stairs. I yanked myself up by the rail and bolted for my room, closing the door as quietly as I could before throwing myself on the bed. They startled me by opening my door instead of Daddy's.

"This one, Eddie," Daddy said, drawing Mr. Lanoux to one of my bookshelves. He didn't once look at me and neither did Collette's daddy. The police huddled in the doorway, watching them with sharp eyes.

I wanted to ask what they were doing, but I was afraid of getting Daddy in more trouble. It felt wrong to have all those men in my room, rifling through my things.

Daddy took handfuls of my books down, stacking them neatly at his feet. Mr. Lanoux helped him, and soon the shelves were bare again, as if I hadn't just spent three days putting my room back together.

Then, with Daddy on one end and Mr. Lanoux on the

other, they lifted my great big shelf—the one Elijah'd torn up first in my dream—and pulled it back from the wall. Cottony brown cobwebs clung to the back of the shelf. The paint behind the shelves was an unfamiliar shade; I couldn't remember my room ever being green, but there was the evidence of it, in a tall, rectangular patch.

Setting the bookcase down, Daddy shoved it around and nodded toward an envelope taped to the back of it. The paper had gone yellow.

"Think we ought to get pictures?" one of the detectives asked, but the other one shook his head and pulled the envelope free. He snapped on latex gloves; then, with careful fingers, he spread the flap and let his partner pull a sheet of paper from it.

They seemed to barely glance at it before folding and tucking it in the envelope again. Skeptical looks ran through their eyes, and as one detective drew a plastic bag from his pocket, the other offered my daddy a business card. "We're not finished."

"I didn't figure," Daddy said, and slid the card into his back pocket. Speaking a silent language of nods and gestures, he and Mr. Lanoux turned to put my shelf back the way it belonged.

Confused, I just bit my tongue and waited for somebody to explain something, but nobody did.

&

Collette stood at my window, holding the curtain aside. "There's only one reporter there now."

Lying on my bed, I nodded. "Yeah, the other night,

171

Rennie slit their tires and set off a whole strip of Black Cats right behind 'em."

"So he's good for something," Collette said. She smiled and let go of the curtain. My room darkened with hazy shadows. Shuffling to my desk, she sat down, wrapping her arm around the back of the chair. She looked at me for a long time; then she said something I never expected. "I'm sorry, Iris."

I sat up. I shrugged. "What's to be sorry about?"

"I don't know. Everything." She traced her brow with her nail, lost in thought. "I feel like I shoulda been in the graveyard with you."

Teasing, I said, "You're just jealous I got arrested and you didn't."

"Well, yeah," she joked back. "I look awful fine in orange. Way better than you."

I crossed my legs, sitting in the middle of the bed and just looking at her. Collette's face was still, but there were all these hints of sleek sharpness. Her cheekbones were almost high; her chin had a faint edge to it. She really was beautiful, and we really were about done with childish things.

Suddenly nervous, I asked, "We're always gonna be friends, right?"

Collette gave that all the seriousness it deserved. She reared her head back, looking at me like I was a fool. "Duh. We're getting out of here when I get my license, remember?"

I nodded and smiled, because I *did* remember. I was just glad she did, too.

&

The silence in my house got heavier as the sun went down. Daddy made sandwiches and soup for dinner and let me eat in front of the TV. He never did that, and I watched him instead of the programs, waiting for him to say something about the envelope or the police or anything at all.

He didn't, though; he was stone, holding an untouched plate of food in his lap.

Chasing bread crusts around my plate, I glanced at the TV, then at Daddy, wondering if I should let out any of the questions that had piled up in my head.

When I saw Daddy swallow like he was choking something back, I reached out to touch his hand. "It's all over now."

He kept nodding, tipping his head back a little farther each time until he stared at the ceiling. He looked even older than he had at the police station, and exhausted.

"You can tell me," I said.

"He killed himself, Iris." Daddy looked over, wearing a bitter, broken smile. Southern men didn't tell secrets; it was a matter of honor. Daddy probably would have kept this one until he had his own grave if I hadn't gone and dug it up.

"He killed himself, and he asked us not to let his mama find him like that, so we didn't. That's what that note was all about."

I hurt when I heard that, and it made Old Mrs. Landry human again. Strict as she was, Elijah had loved her, enough to spare her the shame of a suicide in the family. Suicides couldn't even be buried in the regular cemetery; in a sick way, it was kind of funny he'd ended up there, anyway.

Squeezing Daddy's hand, I asked quietly, "But why'd he do it?" He didn't answer, so I spread my question out a little more. "Was he pining over Mama?"

Daddy knitted his brows and stared at me. "Where'd that come from?"

"That's what Mrs. Thacker said. It was either love or money, and he was too young to worry about money." A chill ran between my shoulder blades when I repeated her words, because it brought to mind all the other ugly things she'd had to say.

"Adelaide Thacker talks too much," he said.

"Well, was it?"

Daddy turned to look at me. "It wasn't your mama."

I tried to puzzle that out but it didn't make sense. It *was* love; Daddy'd just said as much, and I felt like I deserved to know. "I don't understand."

Daddy's eyelids fluttered closed, and he shook his head slowly. He took a breath, then looked up with an expression that told me this was the last he'd have to say about it, ever.

"I tried to make it up. I tried like hell. I did what that damned note asked me to, and I made sure Lee got out, so he wouldn't end up the same way. I—"

"Daddy, you're not making sense."

He looked over at me, broken. Final. "It was me, Iris. I was in love with your mama, and Elijah was in love with me."

chapter sixteen

&

When Ben came to the door, Daddy narrowed his eyes but let him in anyway. Ben shuffled around, stammering, until Daddy said we could go to my room to talk.

"Leave the door open," he warned.

It was strange inviting Ben into my bedroom. I felt like I was letting him look at my underwear or something, which made me feel bad, 'cause I'd actually seen him in his.

Instead of sitting in the chair at my desk, he held on to it, wobbling back and forth as he peeked at me through his lashes. "Everybody's talking, Iris."

I nodded, trying to find a good place to settle, finally choosing the edge of my bed. "I know."

Ben stopped rattling and slowly turned to look at me. "Did your daddy tell you what happened?"

My stomach dropping, I shook my head. A funny sensation tingled down my arms, and I looked toward my shelf, the one Elijah had torn up twice looking for his suicide note. "Not exactly."

Just like Daddy, I knew things now that I never wanted to share; if I was lucky, nobody'd ever make me, either.

"I heard my daddy talking to Mr. Lanoux," Ben said.

I just nodded.

Twitchy, Ben rocked the chair again, then stopped, like he didn't quite know what to do with himself or how to talk to me anymore. "He said Elijah told them to come over at a certain time. That he was dead when they got there, hanging from a light fixture. He even tied a bag of river rocks to his legs to make sure he did it right."

Pursing my lips, I closed my eyes against a sudden flash of vivid imagination. I could call up every detail of Elijah's room. It wasn't a hard stretch to change that picture, to make his body dangle beside the bed, his shadow swaying across a pillowcase dotted with just one drop of blood.

My chest tightened and I wanted to cry again. I couldn't let myself slip into the hurt that had dragged Elijah down until he wanted to die. I couldn't bear to feel it; I didn't want to.

I pushed it out of my thoughts. "Do you know what the note said?"

"*Please don't let my mama find me like this.*" Ben laughed, an empty sort of sound, and ran his fingers through his hair. "I guess she didn't, did she?"

Forcing my voice to some kind of normal, I looked up and asked, "Ben, do you think they're going to jail?" I just wanted somebody to say no so I could stop worrying, even if it was only for a minute. Even if it was a lie.

Ben sighed, letting go of my chair. The wooden feet

rattled on the floor, then went silent. "I don't know. I hope not."

"Yeah, me too."

It was a stupid thing to say, but I couldn't think of anything else. I'd gone crazy and torn open a grave that my daddy had gone crazy and closed his best friend up in. Two generations of Rhameses had disturbed Mrs. Claiborne's rest; instead of going to jail, I should have worried about both of us being sent to an institution.

Neither of us said anything for a minute. I picked lint off my shirt, and Ben coughed a couple times, standing in just the right place to catch an echo in my room. Winding up with a deep breath, he turned to me and said, "So, I vote next summer we don't look for any more ghosts."

I let my feet slip to the floor and stood. Our conversation felt close to over, and I thought I should walk him out. "We won't."

"Hey, Iris?" Shifting his weight, Ben turned recognizable to me again, a flash of brooding in his blue eyes, and I stepped back because I suspected he intended to kiss me.

It wouldn't have been unwelcome, exactly. Ben had turned out to be a lot more than somebody in my way; he liked horror comics and making jokes, and that one kiss had been nice. I even thought about it sometimes. Trying to sound friendly, I stepped back again and shoved my hands in my pockets. "Hey, Ben?"

He opened his mouth, ready to say something, but no sound came out. Instead, his cheeks colored a little, and he shook his head, curling his lips in a smile as he started for the door. "Never mind."

It seemed like a good day for telling all of the truth, and I didn't want him to leave like that. It would have seemed like there was room to talk about it some more, and there really wasn't.

"I would have liked you if you hadn't kissed Collette first."

Caught, Ben had the grace to look ashamed. "I wish I'd known that before I kissed her." Then he shrugged, because that was as simple as it got. He sort of waved as he left. "See you around, Iris."

I sighed and rolled back into my bed, staring at my canopy.

"See you around, Ben," I murmured when the front door closed downstairs.

epilogue

&

Elijah's funeral was nice, as far as funerals went. It was a day of breathing lilies and gazing at them—so many white blooms, wreaths of them ringed with green, and bouquets laid in pretty contrast on his dark blue casket. I'd never seen so many flowers in my life.

It seemed like half the parish showed up, out of curiosity or respect. It was strange to see a sea of so much black under such a bright summer sky. I held my daddy's hand the whole time, pretending not to notice when he wiped away tears. Uncle Lee stood silent and serious, his hand on the back of Daddy's neck, like he had to hold him up. My eyes stayed dry. I didn't have any tears left for Elijah, not anymore.

But Miss Nan did enough crying for both of us. Clutching her tissue, she smeared her mascara around beneath a black widow's veil. There was all kinds of talk about that later.

Still swearing that Elijah was a saint, Old Mrs. Landry refused to come to the burial. She told anybody who'd listen that the Prince of Lies put a pile of bones down in that crypt, to blind us to the coming end of days. She stopped going to church; she bought no more prayers with hard candy.

The mysterious Mr. Landry came. He flew in all the way from Phoenix. He stood stiff and straight until the end, when he leaned down to kiss the casket and whisper private words to his son.

Then he looked past Daddy but shook my hand and thanked me for coming. His eyes were brown, just like Elijah's.

For a while after that, I'd slip down to the cemetery to sit next to Elijah's stone, mostly just to reassure myself he was still there. I don't know who chose the marker, but it was perfect: smooth gray granite, with his name and dates etched next to a carved river. I liked to run my fingers across the waves and dig into the letters; it just felt good, the way the stone soaked up the sun.

When summer turned to fall, I went less, and then only once in the winter, to wish him a Merry Christmas. I kept planning to go all through spring, but when summer came, I gave that up, too.

That stone was just a place for the living to remember him; there was nothing left of him to miss me. There was no more Incident with the Landry Boy. There was just a sad story that ended with Elijah finally home.

It was proof that nothing ever happened in Ondine, and finally, that was just fine by me.

ACKNOWLEDGMENTS

A novel may be drafted in solitude, but it's never finished alone.

I'd like to thank my agent, Sara Crowe, for sweeping in with precision revisions and a battle plan to find Iris the perfect home against the odds and conventional wisdom. It was a glorious siege. Many thanks to Wendy Loggia, a rare, wonderful editor who offers critique, encouragement and line edits; it's so good to have a partner with vision—thank you.

There are so many wonderful people who contributed to making this book. I'd like to thank Colleen and Carrie for their thorough copyedits, Trish for her brilliant design, and Chad Michael Ward for bringing Iris off the page and onto the cover. Big Deb thanks to Heidi R. Kling and R. J. Anderson for brainstorming titles with me. Thanks also to Chief Deputy Anthony Barcala of the Ascension Parish Sheriff's Department for clarifying ranks and responsibilities, and to the Louisiana Native Plant Society for those little details that are so important.

I must thank my English teacher Mary Redman, who was a lover of words and who taught me to be one, too. A fresh thank-you to Estlin Feigley for giving me a voice on the screen and for listening to mine behind it. And I owe so much to Doris Egan, an unparalleled mentor, who taught

181

me how to write a killer breakout, and what kind of woman in the arts I want to be.

My mom, Sheryl Jern, I can't thank enough—for teaching me the absolute value of perseverance and the beauty of seeing something through to the very end. Great, goddessy thanks to Susan Bettis, who always said "When you write your novel" and never "If." I owe universes of thanks to my partner in crime, in shining armor, and in all things mystical, Ashley "Arianna" Lockwood.

So many thanks to LaTonya Dargan, whose advice as my literary attorney I took entirely and whose opinion as my fellow Virgobrain I value immeasurably. Great thanks to Rebecca Sherman for all her hard work in rendering a tight, thin book out of a shamelessly bloated draft.

Thanks to Rachel Green, who read the first draft and said, "This is a young adult novel," and to everyone on my manuscript filter, for your faith and support when Iris was nothing but five-hundred-word previews, completely out of context.

I'd like to acknowledge Blahblahblah, who wants to live forever, and to thank everyone at Metafilter for offering inspiration and procrastination in one convenient location.

I'm grateful to and grateful for, blessed by and honored to have my husband, Jason Walters, and my best friend, Wendi Finch, as my partners in this and in all things. They've suffered every low, celebrated every high; they've shared their ideas, helped me perfect mine. They coddle or kick me at exactly the right intervals, and I don't know what I've done to deserve them. All I know is that they've been here since the beginning, and the one thing I have faith in is that they'll be there in the end.

And finally, I don't believe a book is really done until it's been read, so thank you—yes, you. I'm so glad we finished this book together.

&

about the author

&

A screenwriter and author, Saundra Mitchell penned the screenplays for the Fresh Films and Girls in the Director's Chair short film series. Her short story "Ready to Wear" was nominated for a Pushcart Prize, and her first feature film, *Revenge Ends,* debuted on the festival circuit in 2008. In her free time, she enjoys ghost hunting, papermaking, and spending time with her husband and her two children. She lives in Indianapolis and welcomes you to visit her on the Web at www.saundramitchell.com.

GARDEN CITY PUBLIC LIBRARY

3 1507 00460 3459

1899

FEB 2 1 2009

Garden City Public Library

Garden City, New York

Telephone: 742-8405

GA